Kraken monsters come from the sea. Don't they?

Devora Kraken seems to have everything under control and all she could ask for. Like the neighbourhood tunnels, where she can hang out with monsters and mermaids both. If sometimes it's not clear which is which, that's only normal—right? Anyway, Devi has plenty else to keep her busy, including a good cop, bad cop set of family members. And if all of that isn't enough, there's even a cute girl at the new school across town trying to get Devi's attention!

From the deep waters of the past, something wakes up and marches through Mainland. One terrible night, blood is spilt, and gangs gather in the woods. Devi's cousin, Jon, leaves for the speak-and-listen trials, and nothing will be the same again.

Devi sets off on a journey of discovery that will take her from her home in Exer City across Mainland and into Craw. It won't be easy—her brother Korl refuses to talk about the past, or why Jon left. He won't speak of the gun under the bed or the pile of mermaid figurines. Korl refuses to talk about anything!

What's a monster anyway? Who better than Devora Kraken to find out?

WE, KRAKEN

Volcano Chronicles, Book Two

Eule Grey

A NineStar Press Publication

www.ninestarpress.com

We, Kraken

CONTENT WARNING:
This book contains themes of war and oppression, of children being used in wartime; discussions of othering and exclusion, the use of weapons/guns, child endangerment and abandonment; depiction of PTSD and anxiety

Livi, Ede, Noni and Erk: Don't forget our songs.

Author's Note

The shield children are exploited and used by adults in a war setting. The book is not meant to offer conclusion or suggest redemption but to initiate wider discourse on the topic of how children are treated in times of conflict, what happens to them afterwards, and their human rights.

LOUDER, LOUDER, LOUDER

PART ONE

The Ballad of the Sea Mother

When all-a world goes dark, look up,

To find me in the skies.

Close not thine heart,

Or dim thy voice,

Sea Mother, she shall rise.

CHAPTER ONE

THE NIGHT I called my brother a murderer was the worst of my life. It was early summer, with heat bristling and people noising until dawn. Even the birds didn't sleep. But I'd been sent to bed at ten, like always. Grumbling and defiant. Sick of the status quo. My brother was a stickler for rules. Although I was fifteen, he treated me as if I were a little kid.

School tomorrow, Devi!

Don't forget to clean your teeth.

No wandering the flat during the night.

The usual Kraken rubbish. I went to bed and somehow nodded off. Just after midnight, I crashed awake to an unsettling dream about a stone bridge.

I called in vain for my cousin. "Jon?"

Then got up and padded into the kitchen, half asleep,

with ultra-raw senses. A single light bulb stung my sensitive eyes. A high-pitched electrical scream emanated from our battered fridge.

It took a few minutes to make sense of the midnight scene. Except for my cousin, Jon, every member of the Kraken gang was present. Farlo, who paced the kitchen. Bersha and Tomi, scrubbing blood from their hands. My brother, Korl, and his girlfriend, Anees, talking in a corner.

A gun lay on the edge of the table. Black, metallic, and menacing.

A gun.

I should have asked where it came from and why it was in our kitchen. I don't know why I didn't. Rumours of guns and knives were rife throughout Exer City, but I'd never thought *my* family were involved. As far as I knew, the Kraken gang avoided trouble.

"What's going on? Has anyone seen Jon? I *did knock*," I said stupidly. Obliviously. Trying to avoid being told off. My brother was a rule dictator, and I didn't want to be grounded again.

Korl stopped whispering. For a really long minute, he didn't say anything, only looked across at me where I huddled in striped nightie and cat-print socks.

It was then I realised and acknowledged something was very wrong. Korl's face was vacant, glassy-eyed, and lacking in expression. It upset me. I wanted him to shout the safety of our normal boundaries: *Get back to bed! You don't wander the flat at night alone.*

But he didn't. Nobody said a word. The only sounds were of frenzied scrubbing and the screaming electric wire. Minutes went by. I didn't think of the significance of the gun.

Absent-mindedly, I picked up a cloth and started wiping the table. "Blood. Urgh."

Anees leapt into action and shook my brother's arm until he rattled. "Devi!" she hissed violently. "Put the gun down. Go to bed and lock the door. Now!"

The moments of excruciating weirdness came to an abrupt end when Korl thumped the fridge hard enough to break open the universe. "Get that thing out of here! Why have you people brought a gun into my home?"

His voice was strained and wild. I thought he was about to cry and considered going back to bed. Although I often ignored my brother, it was usually obvious when it was time to bolt.

He blinked, looked from Tomi to Anees, and then finally at me. His eyes went from glazed to heated. When he spoke, he'd regained control.

"Go to bed, Devi. Everyone get out except Anees."

I finished cleaning the weapon but didn't let it go.

Right then, Jon walked in and saw me holding the gun. I swear, every normal sound in the flat—screaming fridge wire, dripping tap, Korl's alarm clock—stopped. My kind-hearted cousin disintegrated. His hands trembled and tears started in his eyes. Normally, I'd have run to help.

"Jon," Korl said. "Mate! It's not what you think. Nobody's seriously hurt. It was just a scrape."

A huge sob ripped through my cousin's body, and he uttered a horrible sound of pain. It transported me from numbness into a different reality.

I hallucinated a soldier; lying in a heap on the ground. Our flat became a large hall, and somehow, I knew the visage was a memory.

"He's dead!" I threw the gun. It skittered, rolled, and landed in a corner.

Next thing, I was locked in my bedroom with no memory of the journey there. I was resentful and angry, but not scared. Jon would be around in the morning to hug me and listen to my childish rants. He'd sort it out, like always—explain what was going on and make me feel better.

I fell asleep hugging my knees by the door and was woken sometime later by Korl.

"What are you doing down there?" he said. "Get into bed."

I did as he demanded despite being stiff from cold. It didn't matter Breen was hot during the day. Once the sun went down, the temperature plummeted. "At last! You can't ignore me forever." My voice shook from lack of sleep and delayed shock at the events from earlier.

He switched on the lamp. "You're so dramatic. Who's ignoring you?" He felt my ice-cold arm and groaned. "Devi Bee, you're shivering."

I didn't feel well. What had happened in the kitchen didn't seem real. Nothing made sense. It was as if the whole night had happened years before.

"Did you see the soldier, Korl? What—what happened? Where's Jon? Is he all right?"

From the way my brother's shoulders stiffened, it was obvious he'd heard and knew to what I referred. "You're freezing."

"What do you expect? You abandoned me like dirt."

It was easy to be defiant. After all, Jon was in the next room and would stop anything bad from happening to me. In the morning, he'd make us hot chocolate and pancakes and laugh about what had happened; he would.

My thoughts led back to the gun. "Whose blood was it? What's going on? I'm *scared*."

Korl flinched. "No need to be. You could do with an extra layer. It's sub-zero in here."

He left and carelessly dragged back a blanket from Jon's room. It was the blue one with pictures of horses, my cousin's favourite. I bought it for him last winter when it seemed the snow would never stop falling. We'd talked about where we wanted to ride on horseback. Because we didn't have much money, every gift was precious. My cousin wouldn't like Korl taking the blanket or dragging it across the floor.

"Won't Jon need that? Put it back," I said.

"He won't need it. He won't mind."

Korl thoughtfully tucked me in and made jokes. He was indifferent to the events of a few hours before and even sang a stupid song about how to bath a cow. It incensed me, but I wasn't ready to broach the subject of the gun or why my cousin had been so upset when I held it.

"He will need the blanket! I want Jon. He wouldn't lock me in. Is he all right?"

"He's fine. I didn't mean to shout or lock you in. I wanted you safe," Korl said.

And then, suddenly, I *was* ready and needed answers. "Who did you kill tonight?"

"Calm down. I know it looked bad, but it was just an accident you shouldn't have seen. I didn't shoot anyone."

"Why was there blood in the kitchen? I'm really scared."

It was true. I was terrified of the blood and what it represented. Haunted by the hallucination. Beyond the fear was something more... A creeping, writhing memory of guns, triggers, handles, and bullets.

My brother squinted and pulled at his earlobe. It meant he was considering how much to say or if he should tell the truth.

I jumped in. "You might as well tell me. I'll find out anyway."

"No need to start sneaking around because there *is* no body. Nothing happened but an accident. Again! Fools. They've taken her to hospital."

I sat up with mouth wide open in shock at my brother's admission. "You mean this has happened before?"

Korl patted my cheek gently. Despite being a stupid oaf, he was often loving and affectionate. At least to me. "I'm afraid so. Don't worry about it. I'll sort it out. Close your mouth, or are you catching flies? Ribbit, ribbit. Which reminds me—was it you who drew frogs inside my leather coat?"

I ignored his ill-timed attempt at humour, although I'd drawn the frogs in his coat ages ago. "What's going to happen? You can't go round shooting people! Tell me what happened?"

My brother placed a flat palm on my chest and softly pushed me back flat. "No, and no. It's gang business, and it's over. I try to keep a hand on Exer, but sometimes I can't."

"You're a murderer. I hate you," I said bitterly.

My brother baulked. "Don't say that. It breaks my heart. Go to sleep. It'll all be better tomorrow."

At the door, he hesitated before disappearing down the hall. I heard him say, "Jon? You want a coffee?"

I closed my eyes and planned how Jon and I could go

into the woods the next day. Hunt for berries. Skim pebbles in the river. Listen to the birds. I shut a mental door on everything else.

CHAPTER TWO

IT WASN'T OVER. Next morning, the flat was empty and quiet. My cousin's bed was unslept in, and his bag and coat had disappeared. Jon was gone.

My brother had left me the stupidest note.

Party tonight. Get rid of the purple chair.

I ran from room to room searching for clues—evidence—anything.

I looked everywhere for Jon. Nothing. By lunchtime, I was desperate for evidence and crawled under Korl's bed. At best, I'd hoped to find a goodbye letter or maybe the stub of a train ticket.

The dingy, cramped space was as dusty as a coffin. At first, it was too dark to see anything much except a thin film of chalk covering the floor and some smelly-looking socks.

The middle floorboard had recently been disturbed.

Whilst rootling about, my hair snagged on a bed spring. I noticed a package in a dark corner, wrapped in a shirt.

It unravelled in a grotesque sequence. Gun—stain—gun—blood—blood—gun, gun, gun.

My mind hurtled to a horrific conclusion. *A gun. My brother is a murderer. He'd killed someone the night before and Jon too.*

As I fought for breath, the front door opened. I flung everything carelessly back under the bed. That time, the spring pulled out a chunk of hair, but I was too panicked to feel pain.

Korl would soon guess the reason I'd been crawling about on my hands and knees—chalky jeans and filthy hands. My brother was a turnip, but he was no fool. If I asked him outright, there was no way he'd tell the truth about what had happened to Jon. I'd have to be cleverer.

Using his dressmaking scissors, I cut a hole right between the shoulder blades of his best shirt. I figured it was as good a diversionary tactic as any other.

Afterwards, I folded the shirt exactly as it had been, buttons up front. Then I legged it to my own room, and waited.

I was lucky. Korl didn't notice anything. By the time he sauntered in—wearing the hacked shirt—my jeans were free from telltale chalky evidence, though there were other telltale signs things were amiss.

"'Lo," I said in a high-pitched squeak.

For all the world like a regular guy and not a murderer, he planted a resounding kiss on my cheek.

"Devi Bee, favourite sister. Are you ready for the party? What's up? You look like you've swallowed a crab."

"I'm your *only* sister," I said shakily.

"And my best one."

He looked me up and down suspiciously but didn't poke for answers. There was no time for a showdown anyway. I suppressed the image of the gun, and Jon, and got on with Kraken business.

The other members of the gang dutifully arrived and took their respective places around the table: Anees, Farlo, Tomi, and Bersha. The final space was empty but for a purple chair. Back when he was a decent person, Korl had painted an octopus with writhing tentacles on the seat. It belonged to Jon, who loved to pretend the octopus had gotten him. I could still hear the echoes of his laugh.

Despite the apocalyptic undercurrents, it was a calm enough party. Everyone made jokes and contributed to the 'fun.'

I watched and waited for clues and evidence of my suspicions. It didn't take long before the cracks appeared. After dinner, the gang fell quiet. They gaped at the octopus and maybe thought about who used to sit there.

By then, shock and despair had dripped into a boiling ball of rage. I hoped the chill got under the hole in Korl's shirt and gave him a cold, if not pneumonia.

"Terribly nice night. Isn't it?" I said tightly.

"Terribly nice? Why are you talking that way?" my brother asked, laughing.

It had been almost twenty-four hours since Jon'd vanished, and still, we hadn't talked about it. Not Anees when she arrived with wine, or Farlo as he hung his coat on the peg where my cousin hooked his bag. *Jon's peg.* Not even my brother, who used to claim Jon was his best friend.

Party tonight. Get rid of the purple chair.

THE PARTY MARKED a new stage of whatever ghastly and surreal phase the Kraken gang had entered.

"Devi?" Anees called, breaking my thoughts. "Where's your head tonight, love? Are you okay?"

The events of the last twenty-four hours caught up and hit me hard. I felt shudderingly sick. I kept thinking about the gun wrapped in Jon's blood. Jon, who I loved with all my heart.

"Sorry. Daydreaming," I said, spluttering.

Maybe my loss of control rubbed off onto the Krakens because the talk faded, and everyone fiddled with cutlery.

"Is it time to clear away? Let me." I gathered up the dirty dishes and deliberately dropped a glass. It broke into little pieces. The clamour snapped the final threads of my confusion. I wanted answers.

When I looked up from the mess, the family stared back through candlelight with glowing anglerfish faces. Korl sighed, but his eyes moved like a ball between ballplayers; this way and that, this way and that.

"Devi," he snapped. "You did it on purpose!"

"I didn't. Silly old me. Butterfingers!"

Just as I'd gathered myself to ask the dreaded question, my brother blindsided me. "Clear it up. Bring the coffee through. You're the Kraken cook now."

"But— No! Cooking is Jon's job. *I* can't cook."

"But," I said.

For as long as I could remember, the first job was

making the coffee. Next, it was cooking, for me anyway. Others could become a bodyguard, to join with Anees and Farlo. Unlucky family members could end up a dogsbody, like Tomi and Bersha.

If you were really unlucky, like my poor cousin, you could be *dead*.

My questions died away. I got the coffee tray and stumbled back to the party, where everyone's gaze was on me. Tomi got up to help and patted my cheek. They took what they wanted from the tray and sat back around the long table.

I didn't know what I was supposed to do next, whether I should sit or remain standing. My thinking wasn't right. Jon used to say, "Devi, relax. You own that body. No need to look like you've stolen it."

The colours of the room faded, along with my choices. All remaining was hollowness, dread, and the echoes of Jon's laughter. I wished I were still a child, playing with bubbles and plastic merfolk.

Korl patted the purple seat as if our lovely cousin had never existed. "Sit." He smiled wolfishly. "Have some coffee. You're not a little kid anymore. Well, you're little, obviously, but not a kid."

The family laughed. I didn't sit. He poured and handed me a cup of disgusting black stuff. I didn't throw it in his face however much I wanted to.

"How's school?" he asked.

"Fine."

"My clever little sister. Fifteen and knows more than I ever will."

He addressed the family, arms outstretched as if

gathering in the laughter and gaining strength from the accolade. While my poor cousin lay dead. Life had never been more grotesque or nonsensical.

"We're going out. Lock up behind us, Devi, and *don't* answer the door. It's a crucial night," Korl said.

He went into his bedroom and came out with an object shoved into his waistband. The family left without a backwards glance at me, where I morosely swept the floor, falling apart.

CHAPTER THREE

I SCREAMED FOR Jon. Shouted and swore after Korl. Sobbed until there was no more. Broke plates. Afterwards, calm anger descended. I didn't clean up the mess.

Instead, I headed for Mermaid Alley—where the gangs hung out. When I saw the Krakens, I followed the loud bray of my brother's voice. He walked with a pronounced swagger, so it was easy to identify him. I was careful to hang back, where not even clever Anees would notice my furtive shadow. The others clung to his side, as hungry for his attention as baby birds. I knew their neediness was because of what Korl had done to Jon. They feared the same fate.

It didn't take long before we neared the infamous woods bordering Exer City. The area was notorious for all sorts of things such as fires, fights, leader trials, initiations, and other nebulous activities. Kids called the woods *the murdering ground*. Apparently, the area was haunted by a gangster killed ages ago, though nobody knew his name. It hadn't stopped Jon and me from visiting during the day to hunt for berries or sit by the river.

The secret pathways and animal tracks were familiar, so it was easy enough to keep up. The family headed along the main path leading through the woods. Miles beyond lay the town of Breen, and the road was often used by motor bikes. It wasn't wide enough for cars, so it was favoured by gangs when pursued by police. We'd never had dealings with the law. Up until last night, Korl's reputation had kept the Krakens safe from violence and harm. As far as I knew.

I stumbled and hit the ground painfully. By the time I pulled myself up, the woody darkness and forbidding trees had closed in.

Grief, fear, and something like regret superseded the cold rage which had fuelled me into the woods. Up to last night, there had always been people to turn to—Jon, Korl, Anees. By Exer standards, I was lucky and loved. Now I was alone.

Sobbing shook my frame. I began running in the direction the family had headed. I sprinted down the main pathway and no longer stayed behind the cover of trees. The woods became alive with spooky noises and the shadows of witches. Despite what he'd done, all I wanted was my brother.

The pathway opened into a moonlit clearing. Away in the distance, voices drifted through the trees. From the same direction, a faint and eerie light glowed. An instinct of self-preservation caused me to crawl into the shadows along the edge of the clearing and approach well hidden.

What I saw made little sense. The Kraken family and a crowd of others mingled at one side of a cleared circular space. At the far end, a stiff body shape leaned onto a tree.

For ages, they talked and laughed while I struggled to stay quiet. The other voices finally died away until only Korl spoke.

My brother held his hand up and pointed to the dark sky. When I saw the gun he held, I screamed. Something seized my shoes and violently pulled. The world splintered.

The next time I was aware, my ears smarted, and I was seated, leaning against my brother's legs.

Farlo ambled across and loomed over me. "What's the kid doing here? You want to play with guns again, honey?"

My brother snarled and then pushed him into a bush. Over at the other side of the field, the body inside the white sack lay flat. *Dead. Killed by my brother.* Just like Jon.

I violently threw up.

"Devi?" My brother wiped my forehead and tried to cuddle me. I pushed him away. He knelt and spoke words I couldn't understand.

I tried to explain, but it came out as a shouty stream of insults and then finally the question.

"What did you do to Jon? Where's Jon? Murderer!"

I was sick again. Someone hurled me over their shoulder. I worried about my T-shirt riding up and if Korl would notice I wore a bra and wasn't a little girl anymore.

CHAPTER FOUR

WHEN WE GOT home, the rest of the family slunk away. Anees begged to stay, but Korl threw her out. He ordered me to shower and get into bed. I agreed. We were overpolite and brimming with unspoken words.

"D'you want something to eat?"

"No, thank you."

"Drink this glass of water."

"Thank you so much."

I got into bed with hair dripping and arms straight against my sides. My brother knocked on the bedroom door. The atmosphere was surreal. I considered refusing him entry, just to see what would happen.

"Who's calling so late? We don't want any bargains today, thank you all the same."

"What d'you mean, who is it?" Korl barged in. "It's me, you muffin."

He inched onto the bed. Lean, wiry, and reeking of danger. My body sagged from the weight, with my arm nudging his as if I wanted a cuddle. Maybe he felt the same way because he tried to slide an arm around my shoulders.

I opened my mouth to start asking questions, but he got there first.

"I'm sorry. I should've explained about Jon. I assumed you knew."

"*Knew*?"

"Sorry," he said.

Sorry for killing our cousin? *Sorry*? The apology had no meaning and was too complex and wide to be understood. When it tumbled from my ruined lips, the question appalled me as much as it did Korl. "*Why did you kill Jon*?"

He jumped back as if I was on fire.

"No! Gods no, Devi. Kill? Why would we kill Jon?" Gently he stroked my hair. "Why do you say such stuff? The hell did you follow us for?"

I wanted to push his killing hand off, and yet it was me who moved close enough to obliterate any space between us.

"You shot Jon and buried him!"

"I didn't! Silly muffin. You're all wet," he murmured. "I'll get a towel."

He was gone long enough for tears to erupt and flood my cheeks and for the floor to vanish and the dark cavern of the unknown to swallow me up.

"Calm down. Hush," he said gently, patting my hair and face. "You need to get dry."

Like a child with a nursery rhyme, I chanted, "Where's

Jon? Where's Jon; where's Jon; where's Jon, Jon, Jon?"

My brother looked horrified. "He's alive! I swear he's alive. Did you think we buried him? He went *home*. Walked out of here. I thought you knew. Stop fantasising and making up rubbish. And don't follow me again. What if Anees had hurt you when she dragged you out of the bushes?"

"Korl— Stop! Shut up. Tell me about Jon. Tell me about the body in the woods. Talk to me!"

"If you'd give me a chance," he said.

With tiny, controlled steps, my brother began pacing. "Jon's left us, all right?"

"Murderer. I saw what you did last night, and now you've killed again. You're a serial killer." I thought and hoped I'd gone too far. He clenched his fists and drew his top lip back like a snarling dog. "Go on," I retorted. "Say what you want. There's been enough pretence and lies. Tell me the truth."

With practised skill, my brother brought himself back from what I assumed was a savage brink. A hooded look came over his eyes, and his shoulders sagged. "I didn't kill anyone. Of course, I didn't! Jon's gone to stand trial. As far as I know, he's okay. What more d'you want of me?"

Korl hated to be mauled, but I didn't care anymore. I jumped out of bed and tugged at his arm. "What d'you mean, *trial*?"

"Craw. Trial. Where else would he be? All roads lead back to home."

"*Craw?* Are you sure he's alive? Do you promise?" Each word ripped at my throat. The relief my cousin was alive was tempered with the conviction he was dead. All I knew about Craw was that it was where we'd been born and was the country where our parents had died.

"He's alive! I said so, didn't I? Craw war trials was all he said. Forget him. You hear me? I wish I could forget him!"

Korl crouched on the floor like a wounded animal, and then I saw it: My brother was as traumatised by Jon's disappearance as I was.

"Trials?"

"How does he think he's going to speak? Well? He hardly says a word anymore," Korl went on.

"He does to me. He talks to me."

We never talked about how or why or when. It wasn't our way. Anees might say, "Jon says dinner's ready," and that was about it. Jon didn't say a lot to anyone but me; he only pointed to drawings, used body language and hand gestures.

Sometimes, a new family member mocked him either under their breath or openly, and Korl would fly fiercely to Jon's defence. Afterwards, they were respectful of our ways and of Jon.

"Please? You must know more?" I rubbed the side of my face where I'd collided with the lamp.

My brother flinched. "Krakens don't beg, Devi."

"Shut up with your doom voice. They do when they have to!"

He pulled his knees up to his chest like a little kid. With a shudder, he broke. "He should have asked me to go with him. I could have gone! I'm from Craw too." Tears slid down his chin and onto the floor.

Scars and wounds disfigured his hands from the hours he worked on construction sites. It stopped me and my assault. It put things in perspective. "Don't cry."

When he answered, it was with the voice of a little boy. "He should have asked me! This is how he repays me."

I couldn't stand it any longer, so I shuffled close until our heads touched. For a while, neither of us spoke. I debated whether to ask anything more, or if I should be content with physical closeness and the knowledge our cousin was alive.

"Korl? Can't you see how much is wrong? We're in serious shit. Why is this the first time we've spoken about Jon, when he ran off a whole day ago? What happened last night? Why are you using guns? Why don't we ever speak about our parents and the war? What's *wrong* with us?"

"Yeah. I hear. I know what you're saying. We ignore the obvious and live in a dream. Yeah. I know."

"What's up with me? I love Jon! Why didn't I ask you?"

Korl cradled my face. "Stop it. You're perfect. D'you hear?"

I pushed him off and climbed back in bed. My brother trembled. The night's activities had caused the scars on his hands to reopen and blced. I ached to offer comfort and pulled up a corner of the blanket. "Get in, Turnip."

He climbed in under the blankets. For a while, we snuggled. I clutched at him as I spoke. "I found the gun under your bed. Why is Jon's bloody shirt there?"

"He got a nosebleed. Don't you remember?"

"Oh. Yeah." It was weeks ago. Jon had bled all over the shirt and decided it was too stained to wear again. "I'm sorry about the hole. I didn't mean to."

Korl gulped back sobs and laughed with over-bright, teary eyes. "I'm going to throw away every pair of scissors in the flat."

When he pulled me into an affirming hug, I was nothing but a bewildering mix of emotions. Relieved, confused, sad, and scared.

"Why were you under my bed? Do I want to know?" He spoke into my neck. It was tickly, warm, and nice. I didn't lose my grip on his waist.

"Looking for clues about Jon. I thought there'd be a goodbye letter."

"And you found the gun? I'm so sorry, Devi—that must have been awful. Though I still don't see why you thought I'd killed him. Quite a jump."

"I don't know either. I'm not thinking right. Why didn't you *tell me* he'd gone? What was I supposed to think? There was a gun in the kitchen, and then Jon vanished. When I saw the gun under the bed... You know."

"I should have explained, but I—I couldn't find the right words. Today's been foul. Why did I say *have a party*? I'm in shock. I'm not thinking right either. And why did I want you to get rid of Jon's chair? I'm stupid. To be honest—he did ask me to go with him. Begged, actually."

"We're both stupid."

We reached a comfortable place of family safety and comfort. My brother was a turnip, but I loved him. I kissed his hurt hands and wondered how I'd thought he was capable of killing our cousin. "It's a sea gherkin. The hole I cut."

"Oh, that makes it all right, then. Go ahead and cut a few more holes in my clothes. As long as it's sea creatures, what does it matter?"

"Exactly. Did you notice it's waving?"

His shoulders heaved with strong emotion we both pretended was mirth. It set me off. With difficulty, I held back my tears.

"I noticed," he said. "Though it doesn't explain why you went from thinking I'd killed Jon to cutting a gherkin in my shirt. You've some messed up thinking, little sis."

"I don't know either. It was panic. I thought if you told me off about the hole, you might not notice I'd been under the bed." I shoved him out of bed and began binding his hands with medical cloth I always kept close by.

"Look, Devi. Are you listening? Jon's moved on. You're going to have to accept it. I wish he hadn't, but there's nothing I can do. Move on. Look ahead. We've done it before, and we can do it again. In fact—we're going to have to if we want to survive. War's coming, and not even I can stop it."

"It's Jon, Korl. Not our old flat or a burned out car. It's *Jon*."

"He's my best friend. *I know*," he whispered.

"It doesn't make sense. Why would he go back to Craw now, when it's been almost thirteen years? We were kids! Forget about the war. The world has moved on! Stop it with guns and blood! Secrets and gangs. Blood in the kitchen. I hate it! We don't have to live this way. We're *better*. Why can't we move? Go somewhere else and start again. You could be an artist, like you want, and Jon would come home."

He tried to hold me by the shoulders. I pushed him off.

"Devi? Are you listening? Stop daydreaming and stop making stuff up. You think I'm mean, but I'm only trying to keep you safe. Don't follow me again! I'm sure Jon will be okay. Once he arrives at Craw, he'll let us know he's safe."

"Keep me safe by shooting a gun at me? Are you stupid?"

"I never did that," he said patiently. "Did I?"

I remembered the sack in the woods. "Not yet. Doesn't mean you never will. You went into the woods and killed! Took a life!"

My brother's face was a picture of confusion. "What are you talking about?"

"The body in the sack," I said, crying again.

"It was a dummy, you dummy. Not Jon or anyone. A shop dummy inside a sack. Why d'you always think the worst of me?"

The figure was made of plastic. I laughed with relief and more tears came. Once again, my brother took me into his arms and didn't let me go. Like so many times, I clung to him like he was a lifeboat.

"Why shoot a dummy? It's the most turnip thing you've ever done."

"I didn't shoot it. It fell over. Honestly, I had nothing to do with it! I think Farlo brought it. I only held up the gun to—remind them, I suppose."

"Of what?"

Just as it seemed everything was okay, he shut down and went still. "The past. Maybe I've been wrong? Maybe Farlo's right about the way we should be going. I wish I knew."

"Farlo's never right. If he says do something, you should do the opposite."

He rolled his eyes, but the fire had gone. "We have to be ready for when the time comes, as Farlo said. The war's only just starting. After the trials—who knows what's going to happen? This time, *we're* going to win. Exers won't be defeated again. Training is imperative. I—I suppose."

"No! Jon would never have allowed it. Is it why he went away? What kind of brother are you? I'm a kid with a stuffed mermaid! You're going to get us killed."

I grabbed the old doll from underneath my bed and bopped it on my brother's nose. It'd been ages since Jon and I had cleared out my childish toys, but somehow, I could never throw the mermaid away.

"The kind of brother who wants you to stay alive more than anything else. No questions, Devi. I've already said too much. You know the rules."

Once again, his words lacked conviction. He tucked the mermaid doll in bed carefully, taking trouble to cover her tail with blankets and brush the hair from her scaley face. When he met my eyes, we both smiled.

"*You know the rules, Miss Mermaid,*" I said, mocking his tone. "*No more questions.*"

My brother fought a battle with his face and lost. He laughed out loud and ruffled my hair.

"Leave my clothes alone? And while we're on it—stop butchering the butter. Though." He pulled a lock of fringe. "It was a fairly good walrus."

"Manatee. You can't leave now. I want to know about the trials. What is it? Is it a court thing? *Why* did Jon go to something like that? He doesn't break laws. It's to do with the night in the kitchen, isn't it? Tell me now? Tomorrow, it'll be back to not talking."

"Jon said he was leaving for the Craw trials. To be honest, I don't know anything about it. He's been writing to someone, I think. Maybe one of the leaders? There are rumours about trials and war. It's got nothing to do with us. I'm tired. Got to be at the site by five."

"You know I'll just keep asking?"

He grinned. "Yeah. I realise."

Before leaving, he picked up my school bag and held it close to his chest. "You've a job to do now, just like the rest of the family. You're a Kraken with a seat at the table, as well as the family cook. It's safer that way because working family members get automatic protection. Good night. Sleep well, Devi Bee."

"Don't sisters get automatic protection too? Next, you'll be making *me* shoot guns."

He closed the door quietly and took my bag with him. I fell asleep quickly, with uncomfortable images of shields, sack bodies, and an echo of Jon's voice, shouting into the night.

AT 13:30AM, I woke as Korl closed my door. In the darkness, I found my school bag, placed carefully on the bottom of my bed. I traced the outline of a new patch my brother had sewn into the fabric—a sea cucumber, waving.

CHAPTER FIVE

I DREAMT OF a mermaid screaming into the waves and woke with a fresh set of unanswered questions. Determined to catch my brother before he left for work, I dressed hurriedly. "Korl?"

But the kitchen was disappointingly empty, though there were signs my brother was paying the price for working extra hours. New rolls of medical cloth and a thick wad of tape spilled across the kitchen table.

I wanted to keep alive the progress we'd made last night, so I found a bright yellow sticker, wrote *ouch, jellyfish*, and stuck it on his chair. It wasn't my funniest joke, but I was relieved and cheerful enough in the knowledge Jon was alive and well. I half expected he might return to us during the day. The three of us had never been parted, and I couldn't imagine life without Jon.

Skipping school was an option, but the bag placed so carefully on my bed, bearing my brother's reconciliatory patch, was difficult to ignore. And I didn't want to be alone in our dark flat, with nothing but memories of last night for company. Figuring the teacher might know something useful about the trials, I got ready and set off.

By the time I sneaked through Breen Middle School's doors, the foyer was empty but for the two security guards. I knew them both well and looked forward to our chats.

"Morning, Eileen and Will," I called. "Nice and sunny today. I'm here and have crawled in from the sea!"

Eileen raised her hand. "You're late."

I was always late. "Only just!"

The classroom was almost empty, and it was easy to find a chair on the back row. Since I'd started a few weeks before, we'd learned little about laws and policies, but I was sure the teacher would have information about the trials.

Only three other students had turned up. The school was academically poor and often half-empty. I'd wanted to attend a different school a few miles away, but we couldn't afford the fees.

A girl turned in my direction and smiled a huge, lop-sided grin. I waited for trouble, but she didn't make any rude gestures.

She stood out from the few others who attended Breen High School. Other than me, she was the only student who stayed until the end of classes. She seemed oblivious to the unspoken rules of wearing monotone colours to help you blend in. With a dandelion of dark curly hair and bright coral-reef clothing, she defied every social rule. Unlike students at my previous school, she did her best to make eye contact and always said hello. It was very confusing. Jon had suggested she might be lonely, but I wasn't sure.

I tried to concentrate on the lesson, but the class was as short and uninformative as always. From the corner of my eye, I watched the girl glance back to catch my attention.

When the teacher started packing away her things, I raised my hand and waited.

"Class dismissed," she said. "Any questions? Ren?"

The girl—Ren—noticed me waving from the back row. "Miss? There's a question back here."

The teacher looked up with a surprised expression. "Oh, right, yes. Devora Kraken? That's you, right? What is it? Quickly now." She buttoned up her coat and checked her watch.

"It's Devi." My tongue seemed to be covered in slime. I regretted raising my hand and wished I could run away and forget about it.

"Do you have a question?" The teacher frowned. "What is it? Hurry, then! Let me tell you, I'm not in the mood to be messed around." She stood and made to leave.

The girl fidgeted unhappily. "Go, on, Devora. I'd like to hear your question. Please?"

Underneath the desk, I crossed both fingers for good luck as Jon used to do. "I want to ask about the war trials, please, Miss. If you have the time."

"She certainly does have time. Yours is a very good question," the girl whispered loudly.

The teacher looked surprised and wary. She sat back down without taking off her coat. "War trials? Do you mean the trials they're holding right now? Craw war trials?"

"Yes, Miss," I said.

The teacher perched on the edge of a desk. "Interesting. I've heard they're calling the event the 'speak-and-listen.' What do you want to know?"

"I'd like to know, too, Miss," the girl said quickly. "My family are originally from Craw. The trials are all Ma's talking about. It's worldwide news. How come you haven't mentioned it before Devora asked? You would think—it being a law course?—we'd have covered it?"

She laughed a silly, high-pitched sound better suited to a fairground. Still, I had no doubt she'd be praised for her enthusiasm. Girls like her always were. At my last school, a ton of girls just like her got all the praise while I was missed out.

"Everything," I said. "I want to know everything."

The teacher raised her eyebrows. "Indeed. Then you'll make an excellent law server." She unbuttoned her coat and removed her hat.

The girl shifted closer until her chair was next to mine. She nudged my arm and then nonchalantly linked it through hers. Such a thing had never happened, and I didn't know how to handle it. Shocked, I shrank away.

"Craw war trials are the first of their kind. The whole world is watching, as you say. Even here in Breen, people are talking in a way they haven't since the wars. Have you heard about it on the news?" The teacher looked interested and friendlier than normal.

"A little bit."

It wasn't true, but I didn't want the teacher and Ren to know we couldn't afford a television and the only time I got to watch was occasionally at the library.

"The world changed when the volcanoes exploded on Skarle and Ansar Islands. Thousands of Ansar and Skarle refugees flooded other lands, including Craw. Creeds fought for supremacy. Some say the refugees stirred up ancient hostilities, others that they only speeded up a war which would have occurred anyway."

"Yeah," Ren said.

"We thought it was over until volunteers started appearing and demanding a new and different trial. People who fled Craw many years ago and didn't get to finish the conversation, if you like. They want to be heard. To reopen the conversation."

"Volunteers? That's sick. Who'd volunteer?" Ren offered me gum.

I shook my head and forced my expression to remain clear, though my brain did cartwheels. The teacher's words could have no bearing on me or my family. It was difficult to believe Jon had left me to attend such matters was difficult to believe. I hoped there'd been a huge mistake and he'd be waiting for me when I got home.

"Are you sure? Who doesn't like gum? It's strawberry." Ren thrust the gum into my face.

"Quite sure. I'm trying to listen." I unlinked my arm.

The teacher spoke to us both with her eyes fixed on me. "People who haven't been accused of anything. The trials are voluntary and happening because of demand. Normally, nobody asks to attend war matters or courts. It's an unprecedented situation."

The girl calmly offered me a chocolate bar. Exers didn't have money to waste on sweets and chocolate, and even if they did, they certainly wouldn't hand it over to strangers. I didn't know what to say, so I smiled and shook my head politely.

"Why would they demand a trial now? I don't understand," she said. "I wouldn't. I'd keep my mouth shut. Life moves on, right? What's done is done!"

I wanted to point out it had been *my* question, not hers. Just like at my old school, the teacher shifted nearer the girl instead of me.

"Well, why is the question, isn't it? Because they want the conversation reopened. Maybe they can't move on? The first volunteer will stand before court to be sentenced in about eight weeks."

All I knew about sentencing was the person often ended up in jail. "Sentencing?"

The girl unwrapped the chocolate bar and silently handed it over. "Nobody's moved on, Miss. There's more fighting than ever. Look at this dump, and we're miles from Craw. Sorry, I mean, look at this school—filled with various ethnicities and creeds. And what good does it do? Ansars only talk to Ansars, Breeners to Breeners, and Perthers to Perthers. Ferns don't talk to anyone! It's a state! Until all the wrongs have been aired, you can't move on. It's not possible."

It was an excellent observation I wished had been mine.

"Ma told me so. She says the trials are a good thing, and there's been enough hiding and shame. It's time to talk. Isn't that right, Devora?"

The way she spoke my name so intimately was upsetting. "I don't know."

The teacher looked between me and the girl and smiled.

"Some people think so, yes. Others are worried more courts will stir things up again. Provoke the monster—you know? What do *you* think?"

"Maybe the monster *needs* provoking," the girl said.

It was the perfect statement, and I was so jealous I could have cried. They looked at me pointedly, as if *I* were the monster! My toes curled, and I considered running and never going back. But I thought of Jon and my brother and knew I had to persist.

"Who will help the volunteers if they don't speak very well? If they're not very confident?"

The teacher accepted gum from the girl, who seemed to have an endless supply of treats. "Thanks! I love this brand." She chewed noisily and blew a bubble.

They looked like two friends discussing a film rather than the painful event which awaited my cousin.

"Do you mean who will represent the volunteers?" the teacher asked.

"Yes, Miss. Are they to stand alone so far from home?" I didn't even know how far away Craw was, only that it capped the far end of Mainland.

"A very interesting question, and the answer's no. At these trials, the accused can invite friends and family and are encouraged to do so. In wartime, facts can get very distorted and blurred, so it's important to get several viewpoints. I suppose the supporters could provide evidence with photos or personal accounts. The volunteers have requested an open hearing. Do you know what that is?"

The girl shook her head, and I copied her with my brain revving like an old motorbike Korl once had. It was impossible to believe Jon was involved with such important national events. My cousin was shy and quiet and ran from trouble. It was, therefore, impossible to imagine him standing in a ceremonial court or government buildings or wanting to be involved. Neither he nor Korl willingly spoke about Craw, and when I had asked questions, they clammed up.

The idea solidified and became a promise... Rather than try to get Jon to come home, Korl and I could follow our cousin to Craw and find out what was going on.

"Open hearing? Never heard of it, Miss," the girl said.

"Each volunteer will tell their story in their own way. Up to them if anyone corroborates or gives evidence. I suppose some might use art or song. Doesn't have to be with talking. Not all people communicate in the same way. Especially people who've lived through trauma. The person standing trial might have memories, but not words. They'd have been young when the war happened, with only a child's use of language."

"Some acts can't be described," the girl said. "Words aren't the only way. Not for everyone."

The teacher scratched her forehead thoughtfully. "Have you heard of Berker Park? It's filled with mermaid exhibits from Craw. Maybe you could visit and find out more there?"

"Yes, I have," the girl said excitedly. "They say every child knew the merfolk of Craw. Do you know about it, Devora?"

I'd never heard of Berker Park, but at the mention of Craw merfolk, my stomach clenched. Not wanting to appear ignorant, I lied again. "Hasn't everyone?"

"Why are the merfolk still here?" the girl asked. "The war's over. Shouldn't they go home?"

"It's a good question, and I don't know the answer. I've heard the artist is waiting…" The teacher hesitated. "It's silly really. The myth goes that until the children return, the mer-folk won't go either. The artist is waiting until after the trials."

"Pretty cool! Devora, we could visit Berker Park together. For research."

"Thank you, but I'm too busy with school."

Korl would never allow me to visit an unknown place with a girl from Breen, though the story of the mermaid artist was fascinating and alluring.

"Pity!"

The girl linked an arm through mine again as if it were an everyday thing to do. I yanked my arm away and brushed off my sleeve, which made her more determined to get close. She leaned a little to the right, so her shoulder nudged mine. When I moved sharply away, she copied and jumped backward as if I had initiated the contact.

"Sorry! You got so close," she said. "Made me jump. Could you give me a little room? You're stifling me!"

It was the kind of thing I might do to my brother to unsettle him. "No problem," I said, amused. "Who gets to decide what happens with the verdict and sentencing, Miss?"

The teacher checked her watch. "Another good question. How come I never knew I had two such brilliant students in my class?"

"Because you never asked. Half the time, you don't show up," the girl said.

An expression of thunder crossed the teacher's face, and I closed my eyes with embarrassment. "I beg your pardon?"

"Oops," the girl said. "Nothing, Miss. You were kindly telling us about the sentencing."

"Right. The sentence is to be passed by the volunteer themself. Don't you think that's cool?" The teacher grinned, thoroughly pleased with herself so many safe miles away from Craw.

The girl wobbled and shook, flung her arms above her head, and then banged the desk with a fist. "Shitting hell! What if the volunteer is down on themselves too much? Or has mental issues? What then?"

"What do you mean?" the teacher asked.

"Only people who're really screwed up would *offer* to stand trial, wouldn't they? Make their story public? Nobody's going to be sentencing themselves to a nice holiday by the sea."

"You're no fool, are you?" the teacher said. "I guess we'll see. I understood the sentencing rule as a good thing. I have to get to my next class. Maybe we can follow the trial of the first volunteer? His photo was in the newspaper this morning." She grimaced. "Didn't look very well."

"Who's the first volunteer?" My voice turned into one of a frightened child.

"Another Exer, wanting to be famous. I can't wait to watch! Almost as good as the football. See you next lesson." She pulled on her hat.

"The man's name is Jon Kraken. Actually, he's a hero. Show some respect!" Ren said.

The teacher shrugged nonchalantly and swiftly left the room.

CHAPTER SIX

"JON KRAKEN. DID you say Jon Kraken? That can't be right," I said for the second time. My hands felt like lead, and I struggled to pack away my things.

"It's what they said." The girl collected my books and placed our chairs under the desk. "Are you okay? Our teacher doesn't know anything about the speak-and-listen."

I found the strength to stand and pushed away her hand, but still, I staggered rather than walked to the lift. "I *have* to go."

"Devora? Go where? To the trials?"

She watched with kind, sad eyes and took my arm. When I tried to sidestep, she stepped in the same direction. "Let me help. Stop being predictable."

I made it to the low wall encircling the school. Outside,

it was sunny and fresh, but I was freezing cold. "I'm not predictable."

"Exers are always angry. I'm not surprised you're defensive. I would be too."

"I'm not angry. Not always," I said.

Then the morning became ever more surreal.

"The war trials aren't something we can discuss without acknowledging the loss of lives and the damage to the ocean," she said gravely. "You *should* be angry. Did you know that, since the bomb, no dolphins or fish will go anywhere near the area? Craw's a wasteland."

She spoke in a stilted manner, but somehow, the passage was familiar. I racked my brains and remembered the pages of a book word for word. It was titled *The Wrath of the Sea Mother*, and Jon had bought it a few years back, much to Korl's scorn.

"I read the book too. It's just a myth to tell children."

She wrinkled up her nose and patted at her curly hair. "*Devora*! It's as real as your bones. We know all sorts of things we pretend not to understand. Even you."

"Will you stop saying my name? Over and over."

"I can stop, yeah. It won't change facts or bring back those lives. I know it, and so do you. If you can see past your resentment long enough, that is."

She pouted like a young child might and stood up, ready to leave. I noticed a hole in her purple cardigan in the same place as Jon's. My cousin had taken such trouble to teach me to be kind and accepting of others.

"I'm sorry. I didn't mean to be rude," I said.

She looked at me sideways and sat back down.

"Everyone should be sorry. When I think of all those

creatures they hurt, I could cry. But it's not your fault. Not as an individual. It's Crawian lore—all beings are united… Or something."

"There you go again. It's out of the book too." If my cousin hadn't been at the forefront of my mind, I might've laughed. "It's the way of the Crawian. At least, it used to be before the city was blown to bits. What would *you* know about it? Not everything is in books, you know. You should try to be yourself instead of some learned professor."

"I know about it because my family are from Craw—originally anyway. Books are good," she protested. "Even you must know that!"

"*Even I*? What d'you mean? Why don't you say what you think—I'm stupid and need your pity. In actual fact, I've read more books in one day than you have in your whole life."

The girl puckered up her lips and turned away, looking beat.

"Your turn," I encouraged.

"Turn? The trials are no game, Devora. The demise of our ocean isn't funny."

Rather than giving myself a clap on the back, I felt dirty and loathsome. After a minute or two wondering how to backtrack without losing face, I caught at her arm. "Sorry. I'm not in a very good mood."

She turned. "I only meant someone like you who's clever and doesn't need to read books. That's all. I wasn't putting you down. *I'm* not clever. I need the extra—okay? I failed my last school. My parents were really disappointed. It's why I read so many books."

I didn't feel well and was clammy and cold despite the

heat. I hunted for a tissue and wiped it across my forehead.

"You're shaking. Is it flu? Or pneumonia? Deadly plague can make you burn up."

"What? No. I'm just a little hot," I said.

"Do you need some water? Let me help you." She fished a bottle from a bag and placed it in my hand. "Drink. Slow down."

"Thank you." I took the bottle and drank. "Sorry about what I said. I'm not an easy person to befriend."

"Oh, wait, don't say that! You're a sweet picnic on a beach. At least three courses!" She smiled a little—almost a laugh—and I smiled back.

"It was intense in the classroom. I can't believe how little our teacher understands. I know more than she does. Everyone tries to live in their own little bubble. When I think about the exiled children, I could cry. I'm glad the trials are here! Maybe it'll make us remember who we are."

It was the first time I'd heard anyone show empathy for Exers.

"Are you still with me? You've gone very pale." She leaned over and brushed my hair from my eyes.

The cheek of her took my breath away, and my fleeting wish to be her friend passed. Exers never touched strangers. I pulled my head back abruptly. "Did you know you speak exactly like a book? What're you playing at?"

She sniggered. "So gorgeous when you're snidey. Did you know? Half undead and half ice queen. Scary and cute."

"I'm not. You've just caught me on a bad day." To my irritation, I did sound cross.

"I kept wanting to say hi, but I didn't know how. Nobody speaks at school. My name's Ren. Like the bird, without the 'double you.'" She waited a bit to see if I'd gotten the joke. "Double-U. See?"

"One of you is plenty."

"That's true," she said quietly, and then I felt guilty all over again.

"Let's start from the beginning. I'm Devora. How do you?"

"Hi," she said shyly. "I'm not sure if I do well or not. You've gotten me very confused."

"Sorry, but—I could say the same thing about you."

Things were looking up until she went and ruined it again by talking rubbish.

"I can foretell the future, you know. Last night, I read my star, and can you guess what it said? Do you want a daisy bracelet? You're wearing plenty of jewellery." She pointed towards the shark bracelet Korl had crafted two birthdays ago.

I held out my wrist so she could drape the flower chain over it, though I'd have died if anyone from Exer had seen.

"Now we're linked," she said. "I know you understand. I can tell we're on the same wave. Do you believe in fate?"

I was lost. No one had ever asked me such surreal questions or given me a flower chain or had brilliant red fingernails.

"Urgh? No. I don't believe in fate, and you haven't told me yet what your star said."

"Oh—so you want to know now? I thought so." She applied something shiny to her lips. "You want some?"

"No, thank you. I'm not allowed," I said.

"Are you better now, Devora? Hearing about Jon Kraken really upset you. It's normal to be upset. *It's good.*

Means you're in tune with the sea, even though you live here now. Did you—do you know him? He looked very nice. Our teacher isn't right—he wasn't ill, only kind of lonely. He must be so scared."

I knew I would think about those words, and everything the teacher had said, all night.

She poked the lipstick into my bag. "My star said I'd meet someone of great importance today. That's you, Devora."

I gathered up my things and was wearier and more confused than ever before. "Thank you so much for the water and the chocolate. I'm sure you're very busy. I have to get the bus now. It was nice talking to you. Bye."

"Don't worry about the trials, Devora. I'm going to help you. Bye. See you tomorrow!"

She waved enthusiastically, and I hurried away, perturbed by the girl with hair like thought bubbles and a glittery mouth as dangerous as mine.

TWELVE YEARS PREVIOUSLY

Shield Diary One
Korl

The Ballad of the Sea Mother

When all-a world goes dark, look up,

To find me in the skies.

Close not thine heart,

Or dim thy voice,

Sea Mother, she shall rise.

This is the diary of how a shield spends its days. To be honest, I hate writing, and I'd never keep a dumb diary except if dying of boredom. Yeah. I'm dying of boredom. There's nothing to do except write, draw, and turn into turnips. We used to be kids, and now we're shields. That's about it. Uncle says we don't have names because shields are all the same (which is stupid). Except Jon, who gets the name of Shield One because he's oldest.

I'm fifteen. Jon's sixteen, and my little sister, Devi, is just three. Devi Bumble Bee because she likes buzzing around everywhere like this: *bzzz*.

I'll never get used to thinking of myself as a shield. How could I? Does anyone? Lead can't speak, but when I said so to Ma, she said I should be quiet. I swore under my breath, so it doesn't count. Sorry, Ma. Anyway, my shield isn't made of lead but some kind of cheap plastic. It's useless, but what can I do? As a joke, I told Jon we could defend Craw by reflecting the sun off the plastic into the enemy's eyes. He didn't laugh.

I like saying the rhyme. It's the only part about war that's good. When we do it together, I feel brave and good. Important.

It's been weeks since we left home. Shields live in the Gatehouse now, with the merfolk gatekeeper. Devi has always loved the silly old stone lady, but I'm not so sure I do. To me, she's moody and angry. I never thought we'd end up living here. When Ma first brought us, Jon was shocked.

Uncle, Ma, and Da. Oops, I mean, the boats go out every morning and come back at night. They lock us in with a big key attached to Uncle's belt. When I asked why, he said it's for safety. How is being locked inside a stone hall safe? Some nights, not all the boats come back. Nobody mentions it. I told the little kids they were still out at sea. In a way, I guess it's true.

We've been here fifty days. It seems like fifty years. I'm bored out of my skull, but I'm doing okay. Shield One gets to go outside with the boats. I want to go, too, once I'm trained properly. Shield One has started showing me how to be a shield. I can't believe he's a better aim than me, not with hands which won't stay still.

What else? My little sister doesn't talk much now. Just sits with the stone mermaid by the door.

I'm a bit worried today. I don't want to talk about it. Being made of metal and steel like we are, shields don't have worries. It doesn't stop me from worrying. When the boats got ready to leave today, Shield One cried and refused to go outside. I was embarrassed for him! I wouldn't have cried.

Uncle was pissed, so I asked if Jon could stay and teach us to use our shields. When Uncle left, my cousin was so relieved he cried again.

"Halt the tide! What are they even doing out there? Why don't they come back? Jon?" I know he doesn't have any answers. I want to hear his voice.

"Who?"

"Ma and Da."

"Shh! The boats, remember. We don't say Ma and Da. No names anymore."

"Why? It's turnip. Of course we've got names."

I want to wind him up, like before we turned into shields. When we had sun and rain instead of dark windows, and when we could spend all day arguing and messing about.

"Because we're symbols," Jon says. "A shield is the Mainland symbol for strength. That's us! Parents are boats which will carry us to shore."

"Turnip, like I said. I don't want to be a symbol."

He sniffs and might be crying again. Now I feel bad. I still can't believe Auntie got shot by a sniper. I keep expecting to wake up back in my bed and Ma saying "time for school."

"Sorry, Jon," I say. "The boats. Where are they?"

"Don't say 'Jon,'" Jon says.

And that's how it is. It's ages since Uncle left. I'm cold. I wish I could see what's going on outside, if the big light of victory has come, the shining light to take us to the land of our fore-parents (whatever it means).

"Will the shining light of victory let us go home if we ask nicely?"

After a bit, Jon laughs. "It's not a person, Korl."

I'm so happy to hear my name again! I wish we could go back in time to before all this started. "Yeah, it is. The shining light of victory is this big, tall person with a shiny head. That's why they're shining, see?" I like it when he laughs, like we used to. "I wanna go home, Jon." Now I'm crying, but I don't let him see. I don't think he notices.

"The shining light of victory is your inner happiness. I think?" he says.

"Inner happiness? The only time I feel so good is with seaweed burger and chips."

"Me too." His stomach rumbles. "I miss chips the most. Do you?"

"Let's go home. Who's going to stop us? We could go home, Jon."

"The doors are locked."

I already know the doors are locked, but it makes me cry a bit more. It's not fair, but I kind of want to blame Jon because he's the oldest. "Shut up. You're a turnip."

"Yeah," he says.

Arguing with my cousin is no fun. The Gatehouse is a mess. When I look at my sister, my insides go horrible. I'm older than her. I should do something to get us out of here.

"We should calm the little ones down," my cousin says. "We can get them to play, or something? I don't know what to do. Please? If Da comes in and sees us sitting here and not doing anything…"

"Why can't you do it?" I don't want to play with the little kids. I'm too worried.

"The big ones won't do what I tell them. I'm too soft."

It's true. Jon's soft as a pillow.

"Okay, okay. I'll do it."

I want him to smile like he used to. I'd give up school, my bedroom at home, and my fishing rod if I could have that. I stand in the middle of the big room and shout. "Shut up. Everyone, shut up!"

They don't do what I say. I'm not having it. I stand still until they quieten up.

"We're going to play some games. Make two lines. Stop being noisy. You're a disgrace to the club."

They form lines, mostly, except the little ones who don't know how.

"Look—can you take care of these, Jon?"

My cousin leads the littles off into the corner to tell stories or something. He's good with them, and Devi likes it. She's chattering about merfolk. About an artist who came into our school, Arker Fi, who made the stone lady. I remember when I used to take Devi hunting for merfolk statues on Sundays. If the bombs have ruined them, my sister's going to be so upset. What else will we do after dinner?

I get the shields doing races and teamwork. When I say, "Well done!" they love it. I like it too; it makes me see how important I am. I'm defending the base, like Uncle said. Being a shield is important, but it's a lot of work, and I'm tired and hungry. We don't get much food. I mean, just because we're made of steel, we still need food.

When the door opens and the boats walk in, I'm relieved. My stomach's rumbling like a train. "Sit on the floor, shields." I make sure Devi's right at the front, so she gets fed first. "The boats are here."

Chapter Seven

TRUE TO FORM, Korl made sure we were never alone together and worked extra shifts, which meant he left home long before I woke up. Much later, he returned with new cuts on his hands. During the evening, he showered and rushed off, or invited gang members in for 'secret meetings.' There was no opportunity to discuss the trials or Jon. I guessed it was how my brother wanted it.

Lonely and frustrated, I turned to Anees. When Korl was busy, I stormed into the kitchen and hid his favourite coffee in the frostiest corner of the fridge. "Serve him right."

Anees snorted. "He's still smarting about the crab you hacked into his favourite cheese. Have you fallen out again?"

"Not exactly. It's complicated. Could you help me cut these vegetables?"

"Oh, complicated, is it? Do you want to tell me?" She chopped the lemons violently with all grace abandoned.

Anees was my favourite unrelated member of the Kraken family, someone who would do anything to protect us and had a reputation for being an excellent bricklayer too. Like the rest of the family, she worked on the building sites around Breen. She seemed to attract the birds and animals and was always popping into the woods with bird feed.

"Stop staring." She nudged me with her shoulder.

I gulped and knew I'd gone as red as a tomato. From the day she had arrived, I'd harboured a secret crush. "Sorry. Can—I ask you something?"

Her body language changed, the relaxed posture shifting into an ever-ready position, feet apart, ready to spring. "What is it? Out with it."

"Have you ever thought how we're—not right? Why don't we talk about anything? Like Jon, for instance, and the past. Shouldn't we talk about it? *Why* don't we? It's a week since Jon left, and nobody speaks."

For a while, she didn't say anything. "What's going on, Devi?" She glanced towards my brother's door. "Have you tried to talk to Korl about *Jon*?" She mouthed his name silently.

I couldn't prevent the grimace. "Jon! It's his name— why hide it? I've tried asking Korl about Jon a thousand times. It'd be easier to chew my way through metal."

She fiddled with the lemons. "There's your answer, then. If your brother doesn't want you to talk about it, then you shouldn't. There'll be a good reason. It's not for me to go over his wishes. It's time I left."

She made to leave me alone in the dark kitchen, with reminders of Jon and happier times.

"Anees—wait? I don't want to be on my own. Since Jon, I'm really struggling. Will you stay a while? There's something I want to show you."

Her tense body relaxed. She breathed a deep, noisy sound of relief and then put down the lemons and perched on the stool with legs swinging like a child. "Yeah, okay. It's odd without Jon and worse for you! I miss him too. I think everyone does." She placed an arm around my shoulders and squeezed. "Staring again, honey," she said, not unkindly.

"Sorry. I'm dozy, aren't I?"

"I'm listening. What do you want me to see? We shouldn't go sneaking behind Korl's back."

Wordlessly, I led her into my brother's bedroom. At the doorway, she hesitated and shook her head.

"It'll only take a minute. It's for his benefit," I said.

"All right." With reluctance, she followed me to the bed. When I knelt, she laughed. "Oh, that!"

I guessed he'd already told her about the gun, which meant she was well aware of the direction my brother—and the Krakens—were headed.

"You knew?"

She shrugged as if the weapon had no significance. Irritated, I shuffled under the bed. After a few seconds, Anees joined me.

The bloodstained parcel was gone. Since the last time I was there, my brother had swept the floor and left a pile of square boxes.

My heart sank. "Oh, no. There are more? I'm so sick of this! He's going to get killed."

"They're beautiful," Anees said reverently.

I was too horrified to answer and shuffled backwards angrily, taking care to avoid the spring which had ripped out my hair last time. "You're sick."

I stomped back to the kitchen to viciously hacked at lemons and anything else in my way.

She reappeared a few minutes later, carrying one of the boxes, and placed it onto the table well away from the ruined lemons. "Open it."

"Are you stupid? No."

Normally, I spoke to her with respect. Anees was quick and strong and didn't put up with cheek the way my brother did.

She slid the box right under my nose. Resolutely, I crossed my arms and looked away.

"You're so stubborn," she said. "Look!" She lifted the lid carefully.

Against my better judgement, I glanced across. "Oh!" Inside the box lay mermaid figurines not yet been painted and without hair. The box was padded with felt and tissue paper.

"Aren't they sweet? What did you think it was?" Anees chuckled.

"A gun," I said sternly. "Last time I looked, there was a *gun* under his bed wrapped in a bloody shirt. Did you know he's planning on using weapons and training some sort of army?"

She bit her lip and drew closer. "Ah. Okay, I get it." When she slid an arm around my shoulders, I leaned in gratefully. "That's why you followed us into the woods?"

"Yes. I thought because it was wrapped in Jon's shirt, Korl must've shot him." Out loud, it sounded ludicrous and ridiculous. Of course my brother wouldn't shoot our cousin. "I know it sounds stupid, but I couldn't forget about the night in the kitchen. Another thing—my thinking isn't right. It's like there's a mechanism which switches off when shit happens. I go blank."

"Oh, Devi. All Exers do. Have you only just noticed?" She hugged me properly. It was so nice I wanted to cry.

"But why do we?"

"Because we've lived through war, and it's why Korl would never shoot anyone! Never. He hates guns and knows the harm they do. In the woods, he'd just made a speech about why we shouldn't be using them. I guess you missed that part."

I spluttered with indignation, but at the same time, I was weak with relief. Anees always told the truth. "But he said! He said Exers have to train for war."

"It's complicated, darling. Times are changing. Most of the gangs think the only way to protect themselves and their gang is with weapons. If Korl takes a different path, he risks losing their trust. You know how he'd hate it. Exer's very important to him. To all of us!"

"What war anyway? Why do people think there'll be war?"

She attacked a lemon viciously. "Because of the trials and what they could incite. For the last thirteen years, everyone has tried to forget, so what's going to happen when the events are dragged up again? A lot of people bear shame, Devi. Those were terrible times."

She stopped and rubbed her eyes. "I'm sorry, but I can't say anymore. Let's talk about something else, yeah? I'm tired of secrets, too, but it's not my place."

But I didn't give up. "Have you heard the trials are called the speak-and-listen?"

As predicted, she *was* interested and tilted her head to the side. "Are they? But why? Doesn't sound like any trial I've heard of. Not talking about it, though, so stop trying."

I sighed dramatically and slumped onto the table, head on my arms. Instantly, she sat back down and stroked my hair.

"Don't worry, Devi! Jon will be okay. I'm sure he'll come back any day now. Korl will sort it all out. He's the best, you know. He cares about Exers, and you and Jon. Can you imagine what it's like to love so many people? Don't ever think he doesn't care."

Her regard for my brother shone through the gloom of the day. Even I could see she loved him.

"Why do you even like him? Is it because he's gang leader?"

"No, Devi Bee. Your brother's special. Like, when he taught me to lay bricks. He's so patient and kind. Even the birds like him." She smiled with faraway eyes. "It shows he has capacity and vision and empathy. Do you see?"

"Don't stop now. I really want to know why you think he's got the capacity to show empathy." I knew he did, but I thought to keep her talking long enough to reveal something I could use to help Jon.

"Don't tell anyone this. Okay? I dream about being properly together with your brother. Having a family. Laying down roots. Jobs, college, all that stuff. Finding out what we're capable of. Like real people do."

Her ardent words were the last things I expected to hear. It wasn't the Kraken way to show ready affection, but I hugged her. "We *are* real people," I said indignantly.

She sighed as if she might never stop. "It won't happen. I know what you're going to say. Don't you think I haven't had exactly the same thoughts?"

"I don't know what to say," I admitted.

She swiftly changed the subject. "Anyway. What else shall we talk about?"

"Craw. Do you remember what the war was about?"

Straightaway she cheered up. She'd rather talk about the war which took our families than why Korl had a gun. It seemed further evidence the Krakens were truly screwed up. "From what I know, Craw was always an uneasy place. Factions fighting for territory and supremacy. The civil war wasn't the first of its kind. They used Ansar refugees as an excuse to fight. But it wasn't really about them. It never was. Most Crawians were—are—accepting people. It was the leader who turned a mess into a war."

Her description didn't sound like a child's memory. It was clear she'd done much research of her own.

"Did you get a choice?" I asked. "If you wanted to stay?"

She shook her head and bit her lip. "Not exactly. Your brother's fascinating. Isn't he? It's profound how he makes mermaids. And have you seen how the kids love them? I saw a group just now outside playing. Each doll is different. He's clever like that! He knows what they want. Because he wants children to feel valued and connected to the world. You know he made me one? I'll keep her forever. She's my most treasured possession."

My brother making her a figurine and thereby sharing his secret was very interesting. I was sure none of the other Kraken gang members knew. He crafted in the middle of the night and kept his paints and brushes under the floorboards.

"Maybe he does like you? He's not very good at showing his feelings."

She shook her head. "I don't agree. Those mermaids say so much about him. Underneath, he's passionate and sensitive."

I gawked and snorted with embarrassment. "He's nothing special. Quite good at making things, I suppose. Sewing too. Really, really good. He's stupid, if he doesn't like you. Stupid and annoying."

"Don't disrespect your brother. He's the best," she said, laughing.

"Ask him about his art. It could help him to open up? Take pictures of the tunnels at different times of the day. He likes to look at shadows and stuff. He says our art is the best part of us."

Her face glowed as if I'd shone a light underneath her chin and given her hope where there probably hadn't been any.

"I hope it helps," I said. "I mean, it might not work? You know what he's like."

She smiled and patted my arm reassuringly. "Don't worry, Devi."

"Ignore me. What do I know?"

She smiled knowingly. "Plenty. You need a friend too. A girlfriend. Don't you? Or am I wrong? I like girls, too, and boys."

"How do *you* know?" I said, horrified and also pleased.

"Devi, even the dog down the road knows you like girls."

"There's a girl at school, actually. I'm not saying I like her."

I settled down and told her everything I knew about Ren.

CHAPTER EIGHT

THE OCEAN FILLED my thoughts during the day as well as at night. I dreamt of seahorses, bright corals, and spikey fish floating timelessly. When I awoke, it was with the certainty something vital had been forgotten. I was driven to craft more fish shapes from anything available, and my brother started hiding the butter, cheese, and scissors.

It seemed it wasn't only I being drawn back to the sea... One morning, a tiny mermaid figurine had been placed on my bed. She had hair colouring and a telltale scowl supposed to be like mine. When he was younger, Korl had named his creations 'sea-dreams' and swore they'd bring good luck. It had been years since he'd made one for me, so the figure delighted and heartened me.

I scooped her up and headed for the kitchen. "Korl?"

But the flat was silent except for the lonely hum of other Exers going about their daily business outside. Once again, my brother had left for work at dawn. He'd left empty paint pots scattered across the table. It was unlike him to be so careless. Mindful of observant gang members, I threw them in the bin.

The reminders of the sea clawed and itched as if something once caged was finally free. I hungered for answers and companionship, to walk with kin, even if most of the time I bemoaned Exers for their lack of vision and ambition. I missed Jon and Korl too. It seemed everyone was somewhere else.

I decided to visit the mermaid tunnels. Before leaving the flat, I pressed out the shape of a stingray onto the soft middle of a piece of bread and then made sandwiches in case Korl returned for lunch.

The mermaid tunnels nestled between high-rise blocks. Nobody remembered who had sculpted the first mer, but there were rumours and childhood stories. Some said she'd been banished from the ocean, others, that she waited for a signal to return. The version I liked best swore she'd come with the children from Craw and planted herself at the entrance as our guard.

When I approached the sacred statue guarding the entrance to the tunnels, I raised a hand by way of respect. "I missed you."

Out of hundreds—maybe thousands—of paintings and sculptures, she was my favourite. She wasn't conventionally pretty in the way of the other sculptures, for she was scaled, with teeth bared and a suggestion of malevolence. Yet beneath the anger, I'd always sensed courage and nostalgia. To me, she was beautiful because she didn't try to please and was just herself.

Years ago, someone had spray-painted *Kraken* across her scales in bright lettering. Jon was upset and rushed home to get a bucket of water and cloth. My brother forbade him from washing the word away. He laughed and insisted the graffiti was no insult, but a compliment. Afterwards, alternative types of art flourished in and around Exer. I preferred the spiky and unusual images and the way they mocked the placatory appearance of the others.

As was my way, I told the statue of developments within the Kraken family. Doing so helped clarify events and sort out my feelings.

"There's a lot going on. Jon's legged it to the speak-and-listen. Korl might have found a girlfriend. She's way too good for him though."

People appeared from inside the tunnel. We nodded respectfully, and then I entered the tunnel network. Although it was early, at least fifty people gazed at the walls, each lost in a world of tails, sea creatures, and waves. Some touched the paintings and sculptures while others stood still with heads lowered. A few laughed and told stories to enthralled children. Some murmured under their breath. The echoes carried and reverberated around the walls. Jon said the sea-like noise connected us to Craw and the beaches where we'd begun.

AFTERWARDS, I SNEAKED back into the flat and wished miserably Jon were around to greet me like he always had.

How was your day, Devi? Did you speak with that girl you've got your eye on? Are you hungry? Now he was gone, I realised how much time we'd spent together and how many of our routines had been initiated by his quiet voice. I'd always thought of Korl as the strong one, but it had become clear they were both powerful.

The front door opened, and voices filtered in. I pressed against my room's door and listened. If Korl caught me at home during school time, he wouldn't be pleased. At the previous school, I'd bunked off often and had been grounded for many weeks.

But it didn't sound like Anees or Korl. The other gang members were in the kitchen. A few weeks before, Farlo had cut a key to the flat. Jon was furious and begged Korl to change the locks. My brother said Farlo would need access at all times during the coming weeks.

Farlo and Tomi chatted about this and that. I considered opening the door and joining the group, but an ominous niggle at the back of my mind stopped me. It was unusual for anyone but Jon and Korl to be home during the day since gang members worked at construction sites from early until late.

Something was afoot. Farlo spoke urgently, and the others stopped talking and listened as if he were the boss. It was another worrying development—Farlo was normally a source of amusement amongst Kraken gang members. Although he often tried to order the others around, nobody took him seriously. I'd always found him to be spiteful, but Korl wouldn't hear of it and declared him a loyal family member.

"It's maybe a good idea. But we have to wait for Korl's

say-so. You know it," Tomi said, easy-going and loyal as always.

"Why? Better to go ahead before it's too late. He'll thank us later. On watch," Farlo said, his command accompanied by a snap of fingers.

Someone—I assumed Bersha—walked in the direction of the front door. I heard the pop of her bubblegum and held my breath in case they checked my room.

Farlo continued to fire orders. I wished Tomi would stop whatever was going on and throw him out.

A series of hard items clattered onto the table, as if thrown. I imagined it to be guns or rifles and tried to tell myself I was wrong.

"One each. Eleven tonight, by the clock in Breen. Fifteen of us. On to the left bank. The winner gets the left side."

A chair scraped the floor. I imagined it was Tomi, who was always a fidgeter. "Take that thing back. Farlo—it's too much. Massive! We're not ready. Look what happened with Bersha. Blood everywhere and another gang member shot! She could have died. Korl said not again—remember?"

"It was an accident," Farlo growled.

"Precisely. We're not ready for arms. Fifteen people? You said it was going to be small? Just talking, you said."

Farlo laughed a hard and unpleasant bark. "It's not a party, Tom. This is *war*. It's starting, and we're in. At the front. At the top. With the boss or without. If he doesn't agree, I've got something we can use against him from years back. He won't risk Devi finding out."

Finding out what? I went cold. For the first time I could remember, the flat felt unsafe.

Tomi spoke up immediately. "Don't be stupid! I'm not

going against Korl. He looks after us! He's the best gang leader. You *know* so! Don't you remember what he did for us? If he says wait, it's for a reason. And don't ever bring Devi into this! I'm going to tell him what you threatened; you traitorous shit."

There was a scuffle and the crash of chairs. Tomi's voice became a series of strangled yelps, and I feared Farlo would kill him.

When the person standing at the front door ran back along the corridor, I pulled the door handle so hard it hit the wall.

"What's going on? I just woke up," I shouted gaily, with a frenzied heartbeat thumping through my throat. "Korl? Is that you?"

In the kitchen, the three stood frozen and still. Bersha squirmed, and Tomi wouldn't meet my eyes.

"Devi, honey." Farlo smiled wickedly. "You surprised me! What're you doing, hiding in there, hah?"

Bersha ferociously chewed gum while Tomi fidgeted with cutlery. I wanted to demand to know what was going on, but I feared the answer.

Using my best acting skills, I sauntered across and opened the fridge. "Shouldn't you all be at work? Who's going to make me a coffee?"

"I will," Tomi said.

"Half day," Farlo said without a pause. "Shouldn't you be at school? Does Korl know you're bunking off?"

"I'm not! It's study period," I said.

They got up to leave. As Tomi passed, I saw the bright red mark on his neck and felt weak with terror.

Shield Diary Two
Korl

We've been here seventy-one days. Longer than forever. I've carved notches in the wall with the cooking knife, so we can keep track of time. It's three weeks since we saw Ma and Da. *Three weeks.*

I'm mad at Shield One. He's sitting hunched up again, shaking, always shaking

"Why couldn't I go and see the victory thing?" I asked. "Uncle said I could go instead of you."

"You don't want to go out there," my cousin says.

"Who says I don't? How come you get to go, and I don't? It's not fair."

"No, Korl."

"But why? I've done everything you said. I'm good enough with the shield!" It's true. I'm strong and true, and all that crap. My aim is as good as Jon's.

"Because it's bad out there. Really bad. Think of the worst times. Now multiply it by one hundred," he says.

"You know I'm shit at sums."

Jon looks terrible. Less a shield and more a bag of bones. In a way, I don't want to go with the boats anymore, not if I end up like him. Ma would have said he's a nervous wreck.

"Do you think they're dead?" I want him to contradict me. I need him to laugh and say, *oh my god, of course not.*

He closes his eyes. "Don't say so. They're boats. Boats are tough in all weather. Boats are our history."

"Did you see them?"

He shakes his head.

"Then how do you know they're not dead?"

"I don't," he says. "I was trying to make you feel better. Leave me alone."

It makes me sick to my stomach. Uncle won't say where my parents are. Last time I asked, he plain ignored me. He's a devil. I don't know why Ma and Da ever listened to him.

It's not all bad. I've got the shields into a routine. Mornings, we line up and have victory practise until they're tired enough to sleep. Lunchtime, we eat and sleep. I'm tired all the time. It's hard when they're cold. It's harder still when they're hungry. What am I supposed to do? I'm not a magician.

In the afternoons, Shield One tells stories, and I draw pictures. We're making our own books from rolls of wallpaper we found underneath the floorboards when we looked for escape routes. No tunnels, but lots of wallpaper, pencils, and even some paint. Jon says it belonged to Arker Fi, and this was her art studio. I pretend she left her stuff for me to use.

And Devi loves books. I like it when she joins in. She's

been too quiet, and she's only little. Shield One mostly makes up stories about mermaids 'cause Devi's really into those, and she has a doll we took from the Ansar house. The one Ma said was empty. It wasn't though. There was a woman hiding behind the sofa. I never said anything about her. I hope she got away.

We've made five books about the mer kingdoms, with my own pictures. Mermaids and mermen are shit, but there you go. War makes you do funny stuff. The little shields can't get enough of our stories. I don't have to tell them to sit nicely anymore. They pile onto the floor cross-legged. It's cute.

Devi looks a little better because of Jon's stories and my mer. I wish I could let Arker Fi know. One day, I want to be an artist like her. Go into schools and help the kids, and stuff. Tell them how useful mermaids can be if you have hope and belief. I never would have believed so before, but now I know it's true.

I'm going to come right out and say this even though it's probably disloyal. I'm so pissed off with the boats. How come they left us here? When are we going to see the shining light of victory? Why can't we go home and get back to being normal? I'm sick of being a shield. It's rubbish. I want to be a boy with parents, and dinners, and friends.

"I'm cold. Why can't we go to school? It's warm there."

Shield One hugs me. He smells. We don't talk about it. Before this war, me and my cousin never, ever hugged. Urgh. I think we're going to turn into penguins.

"It closed down. It's not safe outside, remember?"

"Yeah, yeah. If we're meant to be winning, why do we have to hide? What kind of winning is that? Huh? Maybe it'd be better to lose?"

"I don't know," Jon says.

Shield One gives his food to the kids. I end up giving him half of mine. We're both skin and bones.

"Why isn't there enough food again?"

His hands are shaking badly today, worse than yesterday. "I don't know. Things are tough in war."

"Yeah, yeah. It's what your Da says. You don't have to repeat him. He's not going to know. You can call him a turnip."

"Sergeant. Not Da," Jon whispers, with tears on his face.

Now I feel bad. He's not been the same since Auntie. "Sorry. Sorry Jon."

"It's okay, Korl."

"Who are we even fighting?"

I'm so sick of this war. We had to stop going outside because of snipers. I never thought I'd miss school. My best friend at school, Jarni, is Ansar. Tern is Perther. I mean, we all argued sometimes, but it was never for long. I don't get it—why we all became enemies. What did Jarni and Tern do that was so bad? I hope it wasn't Jarni's family who's fighting us. I can't see it, because he's very nice. One time, his ma let me stay over and we looked at the stars at midnight. It's confusing.

I'm going to say something big. I don't believe Ansars or Perthers are enemies. Not real ones. I don't think it's true. It's just nobody will admit it. I think it's all a big mistake, and any day, someone will realise and we can go back to normal. Say sorry and move on. Like teachers make us do in school. If we have to do it, why can't adults?

"The International Army," Jon says. "It's who we're fighting. I think? I don't know who they are."

"What? Why? No, you're wrong." All I know about the International Army is they keep the world safe and stop big wars. It's what they told us in school. "Why would the International Army want to kill us? We're just kids."

"I don't know," he says. "Beats me."

Shield One doesn't know, and neither do I.

"Let's make another book."

The war isn't cool, not anymore.

CHAPTER NINE

"IT'S FINE," KORL said. "I already know about it. Don't worry."

My brother's response incensed me, and I threw the towel his way. "What? Are you listening to me? Farlo's planning a skirmish with another gang. *Without you*. Talking behind your great gang leader back. I'm sure he's got guns, even though you said no. Aren't you going to do something? He's dangerous."

Korl shrugged and picked up his work kit bag. "Don't worry about it. It's dealt with. And why were you here anyway? Why weren't you at school?"

My face flushed. "Free period."

But my brother knew my timetable better than I did. "You're grounded." He slid a box towards me and took off the lid. Inside, more mermaids waited to be painted.

"After school come directly home. You can finish these as punishment. Use the white sealant. Leave them to dry on the window ledge."

"No. I'm too busy. Why bother anyway?" My intention had been to visit the library again after school and look for more books about Craw.

"So they're waterproof," he said as if the answer were obvious.

"I'll only do it if we can talk about Jon. Korl—have you heard the trials are called the speak-and-listen?" I gabbled in my haste to get in a few minutes before he left for the day.

He rose and left for work, slamming the door in his haste to be gone. I sulked for a while and then left too.

AT SCHOOL, THE classroom was empty but for Ren, who wore multicoloured dungarees and earrings as big as bike wheels.

"My long-lost friend. Hi!"

A group of passing students stopped in the doorway and ogled us. The same bewildering mixture of emotions went through my head as last time—irritation, jealousy, stomach-churning fascination. I wished I were brave enough to be like her, but the suggestion horrified me too.

"Hello," I said awkwardly.

Oblivious to the onlookers, she *danced* her way across the classroom and sat cross-legged on my desk. This contravened every written and unspoken rule in Breen and, for all I knew, in the whole of Mainland.

The students at the doorway waited to see what would happen next. She followed my gaze to the crowd. When she saw the students, she waved gaily and beckoned them across. One by one, they fled.

"What's *up* with people?" she demanded.

"I don't know."

She arranged her many bags and continued to make a lot of noise. A bottle rolled onto the floor. "Oops. Shitpiss."

"It's either shit or piss. You can't mix both together. It's not a successful curse. You do a lot of unnecessary swearing," I said.

She clapped my shoulder merrily and repeated the word, much louder and with relish. "Shitpiss. Who says? You're hilarious, Devora! *Successful curse.*"

I couldn't think of anything to say. Had my brother known, he would have been very surprised. At home, I was infamous for witty comebacks, especially at his expense.

"Good morning— That's how you should greet people. Not with childish curses. You're making rather a lot of noise."

Rather a lot of noise... I hated myself and wished I could go back in time ten minutes and say something cutting and yet cute.

"Is this your law voice?" Ren said.

"Not really. I believe in manners. Don't you?"

When she settled too close, I sighed and shifted away. It didn't stop her. When she sprayed herself from a bright bottle, I coughed and spluttered.

"Oh. We're back to that stage, are we? Do you want some? It might do you good." To my indignation, she sniffed at me like I was nasty and then jiggled the spray under my nose.

"No, thank you. I have no clue what you mean about 'stage.' I just enjoy fresh air and being able to breathe. Why is it so unusual?"

Ren started humming a song, then said, "I couldn't stop thinking about the trial. Ma told me a load of stuff about the war. I've made some notes. D'you want to see?"

"If you want. I suppose."

"You don't have to be like that you know," she said huffily. "Say no if you want. I don't care."

"How come you don't go to the other school? The one across town's supposed to be good."

Her grip on the book loosened. "We moved to Breen four weeks ago. I didn't know it would be so bad. I mean, people told us, but we didn't believe. Who knew there are places in Mainland where people are ghosts?"

She widened her eyes and made a poor impression of a ghost.

"Ghosts don't wear chemical perfume. Or lip gloss. I shouldn't think they swear either," I pointed out.

"They can if they choose to. You need to widen your horizons, Devora. Be bold! Look farther than your own sulk. I don't know if we'll stay in Breen. Ma wants to move back north." She fluttered her lashes. "The students are very rude here. And sulky."

"*I'm* not sulky!" Unfortunately, my retort did sound sulky and childish rather than debonair, which was the impression I'd hoped to achieve.

She passed over a book filled with handwritten notes. "Here you go. This is what she told me. Go ahead. Read it, girl, and weep."

I handled the book as if it were a lump of burning coal. The last thing I wanted to do was read facts about crimes my parents had committed.

Craw is a small northern country with a turbulent history. Refugees from the volcanoes were forced onto Mainland and Craw. The influx created more unrest, which led to civil war amongst all creeds and factions. Neighbour fought with neighbour.

I breathed easier and saw the account was nothing I didn't already know. "It's extremely helpful. Thank you." I handed back the book as the teacher appeared.

"You're *extremely* welcome. You can read the rest later. Ma says she'd like to meet you. Come for tea?"

Nothing in fifteen years had prepared me for the possibility of an Ansar girl asking me to tea. I wished I could tell Jon and talk about Ren.

"Maybe. Yeah. Thank you."

The acceptance popped out before I could think twice. Going outside Exer after school? It wasn't a rule which needed to be articulated. I'd never visited any house outside Exer.

"For real, Devora?" she spluttered in surprise.

Fortunately, the teacher started talking, and the question of tea was pushed aside.

"Good morning, Ren and Devora. We three again! I'm overjoyed you two are present, even if no one else has turned up."

For a while, the lesson was easy and factual. She focused on the process of law, legal procedures, and how facts have to be substantiated.

"That's the difficult part. One person's fact is another's

fiction. With the Craw trials, it's going to be a problem. Even now, factions don't agree on facts and events."

My stomach clenched. While I wanted to know more, I dreaded being asked about my parents' part in the war.

"Ma says the same," Rena announced. "Everyone has a different version of truth."

The teacher smiled tightly. "One of the problems anyway. What do you think? How can the issue be resolved? Fear is part of what stops progress."

It was clear they had both been looking forward to talking about Craw again. I wondered what they'd say if they knew the gangs were shooting bullets at dummies. My toes curled uncomfortably into my shoes.

"Miss. What you said last time, about kids being used in the war?" Ren slipped into bookish talk, speaking slowly and ponderously. "Did you know the army said if they surrendered, their parents would be allowed to live? They were promised, but it wasn't true. The war didn't end with a bomb but with betrayal, which has no closure."

"I'm sure it wasn't lying," the teacher said. "Only a means to an end. Those children *had* to be stopped. They were vicious and wild. As well, the precious mines had to be preserved. A bomb was the last resort. The International Army called it the Shining Light of Victory. Don't you think it's a nice name? They stole it from one of the factions' manifestos."

"*Nice?*" Ren said witheringly. "Shitting hell!"

The teacher blinked rapidly and took a gulp of water before continuing.

"It brought peace to Mainland, ended the civil war, but caused much damage. Craw is still being rebuilt, brick by brick, even now. It's a poor remnant of what it once was. I remember when their concerts were the best in the world!"

She pulled a tragic expression as if the ending of concerts had been the worst thing to happen. I dug my fingernails hard into the palms of my hands and decided to leave school forever. I even regretted having been so hard on my brother, who'd long ago worked out how Breeners felt about us.

"How could a bomb possibly bring peace?" Ren asked. "Ma says there hasn't been peace since, and it's not over. All it did was push the trouble down. One day, it's going to rise back up."

"Does she? I suppose it's possible after the trials, but I hope it will all die out. Most things do."

The teacher settled back in her comfortable chair, surrounded by books and empty student seats. "A lot of things happen in war," she said woodenly, a stock phase she couldn't possibly understand. "Don't worry about it."

Ren made a rude sound and carried on. "After the bomb, nobody knew what to do with the surviving kids from the clubs. No country would take them, and so they ended up in Breen and the other places down south. Shipped like cattle. Banned from ever going back! I'm sure they don't even know who their parents were."

"Yes, that's right," the teacher said. "I believe Exer City was formed in order to house children whose parents were killed fighting. Nowadays, we call the fighters, well—'atrocitors.' In reality, many Mainlanders were involved—from most creeds and factions. Not one or two. It's a dirty secret, but it's true. Craw was a fight-for-all." She looked at me and then looked away.

I'd heard many descriptions of the war, but it was the first time I understood they were connected to me. *My parents*. The daughter of atrocitors.

"What I never get is what did the leaders want to achieve? Where did they think Ansars should go?" Ren said.

The teacher rubbed her face with a tissue and squirmed uncomfortably. "It's not nice to talk about, dear."

Ren tutted. "What about the children? Can you tell us anything else?"

"The International Army found child groups who'd been trained to use guns, knives, or shields. Now we understand it was a terrible thing, but it seems during the war people forgot morality and sense." The teacher finished in a rush, "And now, everyone hopes those children have disappeared."

Disappeared. I pictured the mermaid tunnels made so lovingly by Exers who couldn't remember the sea.

The teacher took up a pen and chewed the end. "My guess is most of the people turning up on trial are those shield kids. They probably have many questions because nobody asked for their opinion or what they wanted. In wartime, who asks kids?"

"But how will they get to the trials if they're banned from Craw? It doesn't make sense," Ren asked.

The teacher shrugged. "Easy. They can petition to the courts. There's an application form. I could get some if you want?"

"Of course! I should've thought. Thanks, yeah, that'd be good," Ren enthused.

When she smiled, I returned it. "I'd like to see the forms, too, Miss."

The teacher returned to laws and historical trials, and Ren and I made notes. During the class, I made a decision. Whatever it took, me and my brother would be going to Craw to join Jon when he stood trial. Somehow, I'd convince Korl. My cousin wouldn't be alone. The Krakens would be together once again.

When class ended, Ren took my arm and pointed towards another part of school. "Shall we have a coffee? We've got things to discuss."

"A coffee? Why?" I said stupidly.

Chapter Ten

SHE DIDN'T LET go of my arm. As we went through the busy foyer, Eileen and Will waved and elbowed each other. Eileen looked Ren up and down and gave me a wink, but Will was more polite. Next time I came through, I knew they would give me a questions blitz.

Who's the girl? Do you like her? Is she Ansar?

Beyond the school buildings was a large annex with cafés, shops, and a few empty stalls. It was cosy, with music playing in the background. Jon and I had visited months ago after my preschool interview. He slipped some money into my hand and nudged me towards the counter.

"Can we afford it?" I'd whispered.

Along with most adult Exers, the Krakens worked on the many construction sites bordering Breen. The work was physically demanding, and wages were low. Money was tight. Visiting cafés and restaurants was a luxury.

"Yes," Jon had said, to my surprise. "Today we can afford a coffee to celebrate your success. Korl has given us the money because it's a special occasion. This school is going to help you get exams and jobs and chances."

We laughed and joked about how I'd probably get rich and buy a boat to keep outside our flat.

"I don't like coffee. Can I have fizzy pop?"

"I don't know, but maybe you'll be drinking coffee when you're a student here. Try it. Who knew there were so many?" Jon said, squinting at the menu. "What a great time you're going to have here, Devi." He hugged my shoulders. "Hey?"

I hadn't understood why he'd taken such care to make sure I knew which coffee to ask for. I'd never had a cake in a café before. The names were exotic and exciting. The café assistant suggested two hazelnut drinks. I chose a cake with a big cherry on top, and Jon got a large, round biscuit.

He was quiet, so I'd sought to include him in my new adventure. "Maybe you could be a student too? There's a university across town. We could get the same bus to Breen every morning?"

He smiled affectionately. "Not me. But you? You're going to have the best time at school here. Go for us both. For Korl too. Learn everything they teach you, Devi. It'll get you out of Exer City. This is your ticket to a proper life."

It seemed so long ago. The memory brought tears to my eyes, and I blinked rapidly. Oblivious to my distress, Ren flung two chairs away from a table and threw a bag on the floor. "I'm starving. What're you having?"

She didn't care about making too much noise and was as different from my quiet cousin as fish are to whales.

Because of Jon I knew what to say. "Hazelnut coffee and a cherry tunona."

She chose a chocolate shake and a nut cascade. We munched biscuits with sunshine bouncing off the table and the memory of my cousin fresh in my mind.

"Look at this." Ren reached into a bag and brought out a stone encrusted with glass crystals. It glittered in the light, like a hundred little torches of multicoloured rays.

"Amazing. It looks like a little planet."

"Isn't it? My Da got it when he was working down south. It grows in the caves, and you can actually pick it yourself, for free. He says there are pieces all over the floor. Imagine that?"

"What's it called? How does it work?"

"It's a stone of inner love," she said seriously. "You can keep it. It's for you." She sipped her coffee, leaving a faint frothy moustache above her top lip.

"Oh, no, thank you. I couldn't." I handed it back, hoping it wasn't a *sticky situation*, which is what Jon said when you ended up in an awkward place.

"I've got three more." Ren shrugged as if giving away valuable items was an everyday occurrence. "Take it, please. It'd make me happy. I'll show you how to use it when you come round for tea. I've got loads." She counted on fingers. "The anger stone, which is black and grey, but still kind of nice, and the love stone. I like this one."

"What colour is it?"

"Purple. If you concentrate enough, it can bring fun. Love. Friendship, with a *special* girl." She raised groomed eyebrows.

I felt my face going red and hot, and my turnip mouth fell wide open. "Rubbish. A stone can't do all that."

"It's true." She waggled her eyebrows up and down.

"You're really naïve."

"Maybe. But do you know what naïve is spelled backwards? Optimistic. It's true. Don't bother giving me rubbish, Devora. I can see past your cynicism."

Casually, she placed her hand on top of mine.

"You can call me Devi."

"Devora is much nicer. Why Devi? Is it what your friends call you?"

I'd never considered the reasons. "Because it's shorter? My brother started calling me Devi years ago when I was little. He said Devora was too big and severe a name for someone as small as me. He babies me. My cousin does too."

Ren sniffed. "You may be petite, yes, but it's not a *bad* thing. How could it be? You're shorter than me, which means you can get away with more. You're plenty big enough to fit Devora. I mean, you've got stinking attitude."

"Stinking attitude, have I?"

Ren giggled and squeezed my hand. "Yes, and I like it. *A lot.* I started collecting stones a few years back. I used to want to do it for a job, after school."

She talked fast, as if trying to fill me in with all the stuff I'd missed during the years before we met. It was ages before she took her hand away and sipped coffee as if nothing had happened.

"Don't you want to anymore?" I finally asked.

"I don't know. Maybe I want to do stuff the teacher told us about, like laws and rules. I'd like to help others."

I nodded and assumed she meant family and friends.

"There's such need. The world is in a great big ugly mess. Everyone locks their doors at night and looks the other way. It's no way to live. We could have so much more. Have you really been to Berker Park? It's on the border between Breen and Exer City."

"No. I'd not heard of it before the teacher said."

She regarded me thoughtfully. "I didn't think so. You tell as many lies as me, Devora. Quite possibly more."

I processed the statement without comment, but inwardly I squirmed like a bag of snakes. "Not normally. You confuse me."

"No, it's okay. Don't get defensive. It makes life interesting."

I'd never met anyone who wanted to help people they didn't even know. Jon would offer a hand if he came across someone struggling to pay for food, but it was an unplanned event. Even Jon never got up in the morning with the sole intention of helping strangers.

"What do you want to do? After school?" she asked.

"The same. I'd like to help the ones nobody likes. Outsiders. People who aren't even on the radar of governments."

She nodded wisely, as if we'd been friends forever. Maybe it was because of the memory of my cousin or because of the way she kept holding my hand.

"Ren—have you ever seen a gun?" I was as surprised as she at the question, which I hadn't planned to ask.

For a while, she didn't react but stirred the dregs of her coffee and made shapes from the pink sugar. For once, her voice was low and quiet.

"Yes, I have. Let's not talk about it now. When you come round, we can chat properly. Man, we've got a whole lot of catching up to do. If only we'd met ten years ago." She sighed dramatically and blew a tissue across the table towards me.

I blew and returned the tissue. For a few seconds, we huffed and puffed to keep it afloat. The tissue was caught, a flighty and insubstantial vessel hovering between creeds.

Shield Diary Three
Korl

The explosions outside the Gatehouse are loud and getting louder. Much worse than before. The enemy is closer; I'm sure of it. If they break through the gates and into this building, it means the boats have lost. The storm's here.

I tell the littlest shields, "Don't worry; it's only boats bringing the shining light of victory." Even to me it sounds like crap. When a little boy shield laughed, I wanted to kick holes in the walls.

"What if they get in?" I ask my cousin.

"They—they won't."

"What's stopping them? Who even are the actual enemy?"

"Everyone else," Jon says.

This building used to be the barrier protecting old Craw. According to the legends they told us at school, no enemy had ever broken into the Gatehouse. It's made of strong stone, and the city walls are high... Blah blah blah. It's all shit.

I've had a headache for days and days. All that helps is when I close my eyes and concentrate. I go kind of blank. It's nice. One time when I came back, a spider was creeping up my arm.

"I don't know anything you don't," Shield One says. He won't look at me, but he knows I'm right.

"You know what we have to do?"

"I don't know," he says.

The shout comes from the pit of my stomach. "Yes, you do!" I didn't mean to shout, and now all the little shields are crying and sniffing. I can't take it anymore. I can't. I'm going to say something now. It's bad. It's true. Bad things which are true are the absolute worst things ever.

This is it: The boats left in the middle of the night without saying anything. I think they've left us here to die.

"I'm sorry, sorry. Shh. Look, I've stopped shouting now. I'm just tired, Jon." I pick Devi up and lead my cousin into the toilet, where the others can't hear. "I'm so fucking angry." My shout fades into a sad little crackle. "The boats left us here to die. We have to do something!"

"No. They wouldn't." Jon shushes me 'cause Devi is listening.

"Why else would they leave us here? We're not criminals."

When the enemy get through, we're the first people they're going to find. Those soldiers will come marching into me, my sister, and my cousin. What have we got to protect ourselves? A stupid rhyme from the olden days and a plastic shield. It goes round and round in my head like a giant angry wasp. I don't know why I never thought it through before now—why we're here. Our task. What's going to happen.

We're going to die.

We're going to die. When Uncle had explained, he made it sound kind of cool. *You'll be the shield of Craw*. I can't remember why I thought it was cool. It's not cool! It's stupid.

"You know what we have to do. We should break out of here and run. Why should we stay to die? We don't even know who the enemy are."

It's nothing Jon doesn't already know. What we should do is escape and go home. I couldn't give a damn about who wins the war. Who cares? What's winning mean? I want to go home and get into my own bed. When I wake up, Ma, Da, and Devi will be tucked up safe and sound. Jon can come too. It's all I think about.

Shield One's shaking is worse today, like one of those old wind toys Devi used to have. "No. Major told us to wait until we get the order. We—we have to do what he says."

"Yeah, but it was weeks ago."

When there was regular food, and the boats were still visiting. It's forty-two days since I saw Ma and Da. When I think about that, it's too much. Waaay too much. The last thing Ma said was to get Devi out. To run. She came back to the Gatehouse alone, after all the other boats had left. "Run. Run, Korl. Get Devi out and run. Never mind anything else. Wave your shirt above your head and run across the bridge to the army. Nothing else matters."

Uncle came and dragged her away, but I haven't forgotten what she said. I don't know why she said the thing about shirts.

"We're going to starve. Is it what you want?"

My cousin hangs his head. I feel bad, but I'm pissed at

him too.

"One more day," he says. "If the boats don't come back by then, we'll escape. Agreed?"

"Yeah. Agreed. We are the shield."

"We are the shield," he agrees, tears running down his face.

"Who wants to be a shield? I want to be a kid." We go back into the hall and line the shield kids up.

"Do the thing?" Jon begs. "It makes us all feel better."

"Okay. Get in line! We're doing the thing. Think of the sea. Remember how it sounds?"

One by one, the shields make noises like the sea until we find a pace and rhythm. It doesn't sound exactly like waves, but near enough. "Whoosh," I say.

"Whoosh," the shields say.

Whoosh, whoosh, whoosh, whoosh. Sometimes we do it for hours. It's kind of freakish. Thank gods my school friends can't see me now. How awkward would it be?

CHAPTER ELEVEN

THE PILE OF figurines grew. Soon we developed an orderly system and always worked in secret. Korl crafted the basic shape, and then I sealed the cast. Later, my brother would paint the faces and tails. He took care with the details like fingernails and freckles, whereas I was bored silly by the whole thing.

"Do you want to paint? You used to like art," he said one morning, eyes red from lack of rest.

"Have you been up all night again? You have to sleep, you know."

He rubbed his head wearily. "We have to get them finished and delivered before it's too late."

"What are you talking about? There's no rush. Nobody *needs* a mermaid doll." I was sick of the creepy things and of spending any spare minute in sealing chalk. My hands were sore and so was my temper.

"Surprising I'm able to function at all, since I'm a sisiutl." I eyed the butter, a nice, new slab ripe for kitchen art.

Korl snatched up the pack and wouldn't let it go. "What's a sisiutl?"

"Double-headed sea serpent. Don't you know anything? One of my heads is a schoolgirl. The other is the sister of a gun-wielding gangster. No wonder I'm confused, but no. There's no need for you to feel guilty."

He opened his mouth to retaliate and then clamped it shut. Despite my valiant efforts to goad my brother, he remained aloof.

"Nothing double-headed about you, Devi. You've one head and it's grumpy. I didn't go to school, remember? Because I had to work to keep us alive. *That*'s why I don't know the name of every fish."

Guilt was me. From the corner of my eye, I noticed new and untreated cuts on his hands from working too many hours on dangerous construction sites.

"Let me bind you. It looks so sore." I rose to get the medical supplies.

My brother held out his hands in readiness and allowed me to bathe and clean the wounds. I spent longer than normal and made sure to rub soothing cream into his rough skin. When it was done, I kissed his wrist and sensed his intense scrutiny.

"You need to take better care of yourself," I said. "How do you paint faces with hands like these?"

His shoulders sagged and some of the tightness of his body relaxed. "No choice. Not if we want to eat. Things are even tighter now Jon's left. Um, Devi? Where did you hear the trials are called the speak-and-listen? What is it?"

"At school. The teacher says it's the first one. The volunteers—like Jon—can say whatever they want in any way they choose. It's supposed to be about conversation and not punishment. 'Trial' is actually not a very useful description, is it?"

He stared. "Speak-and-listen. Really?"

Surprised and pleased at his interest, I decided to push my luck. "Yeah. Can we talk now? I'm worried and don't know what to do."

"I've only got a few minutes before work," he said warily.

"We can't keep looking away from important things. What's going on with Farlo and the gangs? You can't ignore it and hope it'll go away. Tell me about the night with the blood. It's why Jon went, isn't it?"

He sighed and pulled his hands away. "I can't sort everything out. I'm trying my best! Have you considered that maybe I'm not the villain you think? Can't make the right decisions. I don't *know* how to protect my people or do what's best. Can you guess how small it makes me feel? I'm rubbish."

It was the most shocking thing my brother had ever said, at least to me. He sounded defeated and lost instead of the gang leader I knew. Without time to prepare, the switch in power was too much to handle.

"Don't say you're rubbish! It's not true. Let me help! I only want to talk," I said after a long pause bristling with tension.

He closed his eyes. "Nothing to tell. Like I said at the

time. You're late for school."

"Never mind about school! Our cousin's missing and needs our help, and you won't even talk about it! Maybe we should be going to the trial too? Gods know we need to speak and listen! All you do is waste time showing off with guns. If you don't talk to me, I'm going to leave you and go after Jon. Then you'll be all alone. Do you even care?"

I shouted much louder than was necessary. My brother grabbed his coat and left without taking the hand salve or the sandwiches I'd made. The door banged in his wake.

A few minutes later, I locked up and left the flat too. By the time the bus reached Breen, I'd just about stopped swearing but couldn't forget the haunted look on my brother's face or how he'd cowered.

A newsstand banner claimed to have personal stories of the war trials. When the seller saw my interest, she waved the paper towards me. "Read all about it—the merfolk of Craw coming home!"

I entered school expecting everything to be the same as ever. Instead, a poster. *War Trials: The Final Reckoning*. It seemed the whole of Mainland was caught up in the trials.

As I dithered, two figures cornered me. "Hey, Devora!"

"Stop avoiding us!" Will said. "You've got something to tell."

"Don't try to escape us, or he might use his whispering skills on you. Tell!" Eileen poked me. "Who's the darling?"

"You mean Ren?"

"Go on." Eileen prodded my foot with her shoe. "She's in the same course as you?"

"Yeah."

"Wonderful." Eileen looked like she might cry. "At last!

For the last five years since starting this job, I turn up for work and hope I'll see it."

"My lovely face?" Will handed us each a drink.

Eileen snorted and opened her can. "I see your lovely face all right, Will. It's not the issue. What I don't see—" She paused and took a swig of her drink. "Development."

"Ah. True. No, we don't see a lot of that," Will said sadly.

I drank. Orange bubbles of opulence hit my taste buds. "What kind of development?"

"Mixing. Kids making friends. Exers talking to Ansars, Perthers, and Breener kids. Dates and couples. Friends. Those kinds of developments. We don't see it. Not at all. Not ever. If anything, things are going the other way."

"Oh. Yeah. I see what you mean."

Will drank the contents of his can in one gulp. "Until now. I knew it would be you, Devora. You're the one."

I gulped the drink. The orange bubbles, the sun shining onto my face, and the reminders of Jon made me lose control of my mouth. "The one what? Ren's Ansar. She says her family only just moved to Breen. It's too complicated. You can't ignore facts. Ansars think Exers are animals. We should be enemies."

"Did you know love is one of the strongest forces? The other is the sea," Will said.

"Love? Blurgh! Sometimes I don't even like her."

"Oh, love's always like that," Will said.

I didn't mean to mention it, but Korl was in my mind, and somehow the question tumbled out anyway. "Have *you* ever used a gun?"

They looked at each other and then at me. Will whistled low. "A gun. What's up?"

By the change in their demeanour it was clear I'd made a mistake. There was no easy way to backtrack, so I pressed the button for the lift. "Nothing. It's something for class. Bye!"

I stepped into the lift quickly and looked away from their worried expressions.

The classroom was empty but for Ren, who jumped up. She rushed forward, excited to see me like nobody except Jon had ever been.

"You're here! I was so worried you wouldn't come today. Thank gods you did. I might *have* to give you a big kiss." She skipped across the classroom and hugged me.

"I'm pleased to see you too," I said a little stiffly. "Very pleased."

She beamed and gripped my hand. "Better! Last time, what did you say? Was it good morning, like an old news reader? Something like that."

As exuberant as ever, she pulled me onto a chair. "Do you like this?" She thrust her wrist into my face, revealing a shiny black glittering armband.

"Nice. What stones are they?" I asked.

"I knew you'd like it! Those are the secrets stones. There's no teacher today. All she left is a dumb note. 'Lesson cancelled today due to unforeseen circumstances.' You know what? It means she couldn't face it and probably got drunk last night."

"That's quite an assumption! A note?" I said.

"Yeah. Because she knows *we'll* be here, even if nobody else is." Ren linked her arm through mine. "Shall we walk through town? Might as well get out of this dump."

"Why do you do this?" I asked, looking down at her arm.

"One day, you'll get it. But you won't find the answer in a book," she replied.

We strolled into the town centre, where many people sat outside restaurants drinking strong-smelling coffee or tall glasses of beer. They clearly had money to spend and time to waste. For some reason, I thought of my brother toiling with bricks and wished we'd not argued.

"Why is life so difficult?" I said. "The trials seem far away. I wish it was all over, and we could go back to normal." We had never been normal.

"I know what you mean. Don't you find a lot of stuff like that? Ma talks about Craw all the time." Ren looked at me sideways. "If I tell you something, do you promise you won't get angry?"

"Yeah. I guess."

"To tell you the truth, I used to be very jealous of you."

The concept was as incomprehensible as a mountain wishing it were a tree. "Say it again. *You*, jealous of *me*? But you've got everything. A family. A home and a city." I trailed off.

She frowned and wrinkled up her nose. "So have you. You've got most of those things too."

The old familiar bitterness flared, and I bit my lip. I knew—or thought I knew—there was no point in explaining the difference between her home and mine. I guessed she wouldn't know of the constant fear and guilt Exers carried, and there was no way I could explain we woke up knowing our parents had been killers.

"Have I upset you?" she said after a minute or two. "I didn't mean to. I'm only trying to be honest. You told me something important last time, so I'm doing the same.

Something real."

"Why were you jealous of *me*?"

"Because you've got a whole city of people to identify with. You can be with other Exers and reminisce, have dates, and friends. Don't you live in gangs, like Ma says? I wish I lived amongst my people, but I don't, and I can't. Ansars don't belong anywhere."

I considered how she perceived Exer City. The Krakens did all the things she described, yet I'd never thought of us in that way.

"I was jealous of you too," I said. "Really jealous. I thought you had everything."

"I've always wanted to bring a friend home. Have you?"

"No. I never even thought about it. It's the difference between Exers and you. There are so many things I haven't considered. I always assumed we couldn't do things, and now I don't know why."

We trailed past shops and stalls. Any minute, I expected to be stopped by law enforcers, but nobody stopped us or asked why I was so far out of Exer City. There were no actual laws preventing me from being there, only fear and superstition.

One café was surrounded by sculptures in various costumes and poses.

"Look," I said. "Have you seen this? My brother would love this."

Ren grinned. "It's famous. You're staring like it's the zoo. I was the same the first time I came here. According to Breen legends, the one you pick is meant to say a lot about who you are. First time we came, I chose this one." She pointed to a tall marble figure with golden wings.

"Why her?"

"I want to see everything! Go everywhere. Fly, and always keep looking. I don't have a home except my wings. Which one are you, Devora?"

Two statues caught my eye. The first was a metallic gun with arms and legs but no head.

"It's called the Human Bullet," Ren said.

"Like me? I don't know who I am or much about my past, but I suppose I was from one of the clubs the teacher told us about. Is it the one you wanted me to see? Because of what I said about the gun?"

"No. I don't want to talk about guns because they're part of my past too. I'm from Craw, just like you."

"Not just like me. Ansars weren't in child clubs."

"This is the one I wanted you to see." Ren led me to another stature standing apart from the others.

It was a monster dressed in seaweed, with long claws and tentacles for hair. She was dressed in rags and yet gleamed from tiny, encrusted gems. The combination of styles reminded me of the Kraken beast.

"She's like one of the statues in Exer," I said.

"I know the one you mean!" Ren touched the base of the beast gently and held its foot. "This one has a long journey ahead. She's far from home."

"She doesn't care if she looks good or not."

"It's why I think she's dignified." Ren pulled me around to the other side, where the monster appeared to be dancing. "It's all a matter of perspective."

Shield Diary Four
Korl

I don't want to write this. They took Jon. They've taken my cousin! I keep telling Devi they've taken him to the shops or something, but they haven't. They've taken him to fight. I tried to stop Uncle! I told him Shields don't shoot guns. He didn't listen. Jon's gone. It's too much to get my head round.

I've lost my whole family except little Devi. She won't let go of my hand, and I won't let go of her. Not ever. I keep thinking about what Ma said about getting out. I'm so fucking angry. I've punched holes in every patch of wall. I'm still angry and it's going to last until the end of time. I could rip Uncle's head right off his neck with my hands. I'm angry and sad. It goes round in my head. Angry and sad, angry and sad, angry and sad. How does so much feeling not cause a big hole in the universe?

I should have done something earlier. I told Ma and Da ages ago, back when Uncle started coming round. "He's horrible. There's nothing wrong with Ansars, or Perthers. It's not their fault Craw is a mess. Why can't you all talk to one another? Why blame Ansars?"

They didn't listen to me. Nobody listened. I'm going to explode. All that keeps me sane is the mermaid book.

I draw around one of the punch holes I've made in the wall. "Look, Devi—It's a mermaid." She comes to look, and then all the shields start drawing merfolk on the walls. "Let's read a story."

We huddle under the stone lady. Devi sits on her feet and sings. I've started talking to that mermaid. How strange I've gone. Sometimes, I swear she hears me and answers in the voice of Arker Fi.

"Korl," she says. "I remember you. I'm here."

We don't have Jon, but we have the voice of Arker Fi and some food. Enough to last a few weeks. I've rationed it out and put it on a shelf too high for the kids to reach. I know all their tricks. I invented most of the tricks myself! Hah.

Without Jon, everything's fallen apart. I keep trying to line the shields up, like I'm supposed to, but they whine and cry and then I get mad-sad.

"Where's Shield One? I want my ma," they cry, and it finishes me.

I keep thinking how Jon was going to pieces even before they made him hold a gun and shoot. His hands were shaking so bad. He *knew*, I'm sure. He knew they'd make him. Maybe they made him shoot before, and he never told me because he wanted to save me and Devi?

He won't stand a chance out there. He volunteered so we didn't have to. I know it. When I think about him dead, I go blank. I just go. Yesterday, I lost hours doing it, and the kids asked me how. I told them, think of home. One by one, they all went quiet and kind of blank. The silence stayed in my head. It's creepy but silent. It's not nice or bad.

"It's the creeps," the kids say. "The creeps got him."

When we were the little kids, Jon and I used to go down to the river and make fishing rods out of reeds. One time, we caught a big fish and took it home for Ma to cook for dinner.

I'm not going to cry. What's the point? What's the point of it? I'm not going to, not going to.

CHAPTER TWELVE

THE TRIAL DATE inched closer, and consequently, I couldn't keep up with the frantic pace or the changes to our regular routine. As the rest of the world sped up, I became slower than a starfish. My worries about Jon morphed from intense pain into a dull ache. Instead of panicked nights, I fell asleep quickly and only woke when Korl shouted.

"What's the rush?" I grumbled.

Elsewhere, the cloud of tension built with the smouldering summer heat. In Exer City, shops closed much earlier than they used to, and people stayed inside. On the hottest days, the streets were quiet rather than filled with children playing. Even the normally busy merfolk tunnels were silent and empty.

The mermaid army grew impressively big, and as it did,

my brother started to relax. Each morning, a new batch waited in a box by the door, either blank clones or intricately painted.

"Why more? Don't you ever sleep? What are you grinning at?" I asked.

"You, Devi! The way you're scowling at the figures. Did you know you look exactly like the Kraken mermaid?"

I offered my sternest glare, but it wasn't enough to suppress his grin. He planted a loud and sticky kiss on my cheek and giggled like a child.

"I want to make sure all the children have one, and it's starting to look possible. No child should be without hope. The scarf looks good, Devi Bee. Very chic." He yawned with tired eyes and deftly tied the crinkled cloth draped loosely around my neck.

"What are you so cheery about all of a sudden? I'm not used to it!"

"Cheeky." He kissed my cheek again and—for once—made me sandwiches instead of the other way round. When I opened the packet, I found a biscuit cut into the shape of a star fish.

School remained far behind the rest of the world with nothing much changing. Until one morning, a teacher ripped down a banner giving details of the trials. When he noticed me watching, he threw it onto the floor and scuttled off without looking back.

"What's going on?" I asked Eileen, who stood by the doors, arms crossed. "Did you see?"

"I saw. They're scared."

"Of the trial?"

"Of what it might bring. They remember what

happened during the war and afterwards." She took my arm and led me to the office she shared with Will. "How long till class?"

"Oh, ages yet. I'm early."

"You, early?" She feigned shock.

"I know! It's because there was no hold-up at the bus station. Normally it takes at least half an hour to get through, but today it's empty. Things are strange, Eileen. Where is everyone? What are they scared of? Craw's miles from here, and anyway, these things happened years ago. Have you always lived here?"

"No, no. I'm from Craw. Actually, a lot of the staff are from the north. I came to Breen with Will during the exodus. Before the bomb, thank gods."

"I didn't realise! Tell me about the Craw war and Breen—you must know loads. How can Craw impact a country so far away? I don't get it."

"Well, I guess you could say the tension between factions in the wars was finance-driven. In Breen anyway. Perthers have legal control of the mines. There was unrest about wages, which led to fighting amongst creeds. Just like with Craw—except in Breen, the politicians dealt with the unrest harshly."

Will appeared. He winked and sat on the back of Eileen's chair. "You talking about the demonstrations last night? Breeners demand the right to speak. People won't be silenced forever. The speak-and-listen is sweeping Mainland."

"I don't see why everyone else has to be involved with Craw. Why can't people follow their own lead instead of waiting for others to do it?"

Eileen and Will's descriptions of the Breen wars filled me with apprehension. Whatever happened to Jon was linked to the rest of the world. There'd be trouble all over. My cousin would have hated it.

"Nobody knows what's going to happen, but the wheels are definitely turning," Eileen said. "We hope there won't be a war of weapons but an explosion of words. You'll be late for class though. You better go, Devi."

They walked me to the lifts. As I pressed the button, Will took my elbow and whispered loudly. "When you get to Craw, Devi, where are you going to stay? There's a list of free accommodations here. The courts will pay for Exers and other children of the war. It's free."

He slipped a sheet of paper into my pocket. "There are some nice places by the sea. You'll like it. Not in Craw, of course. Not until they sort out the water troubles."

"What?" I whipped around. "How do you know *I'm* going to Craw?"

He patted my shoulder. "I'm not as stupid as I look. It's obvious you're going to the speak-and-listen."

"Because of Jon Kraken," Eileen said. "He's the man you came with on the day of your interview, right? We saw you in the café. Is he a brother or cousin?"

"You know? You knew all along?"

"'Course we know," Eileen said. "You're the first Exer to study here, and you're taking law. Don't you know how significant that is? It's obvious *you're* going to the speak-and-listen and it's your family who started it."

"Jon's my cousin. I don't know what's going to happen to him. I don't know anything."

"The thing is," Will said, "I can't go back to my real

home. Skarle Island isn't habitable anymore. But you can. I know it won't be easy."

"Stop it, Will. She's not ready," Eileen said.

The lift arrived, and people spilled out. I hurried inside, sniffing. I went up and down in the lift until I could control my emotions. By the time I reached the classroom, at least five more posters had appeared on the walls and windows. If Ren hadn't been waiting outside the classroom, I might well have gone home. She saw me and waved enthusiastically.

"Devora!"

Shield Diary Five
Korl

Jon's back! He's alive. Whatever happens now, I'll be grateful and happy, and I won't complain again. It was four days. Uncle threw him in and then locked the door back up before I could rip his head off.

Poor Jon. Poor, poor Jon. A wound in the leg and in so much pain. I don't know what to do. I've tied up his leg with a shirt, the way Ma showed me. It looks like a bullet went right through. We don't have anything; no medicine. Nothing except kids, plastic shields, and me.

My heart's yammering so fast it feels like it's going to fly through my chest. I keep thinking about escaping or doing something worse. What stops me is Devi. She's sitting with Jon's head on her lap, singing songs about mermaids.

"Can we do the sea thing?" Arlo asks. "Can I be in your family?"

"Yeah, Arlo," I say. "Sure thing. We'll make a Kraken gang. Okay. Line up."

We make sea noises. It turns into a sort of song. It's nice and soothing. I'm glad my friends from school can't see me now.

I'm working on a plan. It's not one Jon would ever agree to, but he's in too much pain to care.

CHAPTER THIRTEEN

WHEN REN PULLED me into a hug, it was me who held on and made it last. Whatever happened in Breen and Craw, she alone was unchanged, and her welcome was guaranteed.

"No teacher again?" I asked, though I didn't care about her absence and welcomed the chance to spend time with my friend.

"No, but never mind. You're about to take a chance, Devora, though you wouldn't agree with my assessment."

"A chance on what?"

"To visit Berker Park. We can talk about the trial. Shall we?"

"Well, but maybe the teacher will show? She's not so late."

"Don't be scared. Come. We'll take a picnic. You need to

take more risks." She offered a manicured hand, which I took.

We walked through empty school corridors and into vibrant Breen with my hip occasionally bumping hers.

Under the midday sunshine, we puffed and panted until finally arriving at a gate flanked on either side by stone lions. From what I could see, the park had known better days. The grasses were uncut and the paint on the wall chipped.

I didn't want to appear ungrateful, so I smiled and tried to appear excited. "It looks great!"

"I know you're going to love it. There's something you'll be very interested in." She wiped her forehead and made a fan from her hand. "It's too hot!"

The spectacle beyond the gate was so unexpected it took a few moments for my eyes to adjust. A meadow lay beyond, bursting with rows of brilliantly coloured flowers and trees of every kind. Dotted about were strange sculptures of animals and birds. A long lake shimmered in the distance, as brilliant as a visage from a painting. A few other people strolled or sat upon the grass, but otherwise, we had the place to ourselves.

"Well?" Ren demanded.

"I've never seen anything like it."

Although only a mile away, the park seemed another world away from either Breen or Exer City. The fields and lakes teemed with exotic birds, multicoloured butterflies, and strange and wonderful plant life I'd never seen elsewhere.

Tall flowers as high as a human and fields of red-and-blue grasses. A flowing river gushed past, banked by reeds and nesting birds. Tiny boats moored and attached to islands and banks. The gentle but insistent sway of the boats jolted a memory, just beyond my grasp.

"Is it the sea?" I asked.

Ren laughed at my astonishment and led me onto a winding pathway. "Wait until you see the exhibits. If you think this is good, get ready to be knocked off your feet, Devora!"

We reached statues and sculptures of wind machines and freaky and fantastical echo makers. I stopped at every piece to examine the materials and the shapes and the way the light cast shadows. I thought constantly of Korl and wished I could bring him here.

"I knew you'd like it," Ren said. "The first time we met, I thought, I'm taking her to Berker Park."

"Why?"

"Books are good. What's in the heart is better." She dropped her bags. Amidst wind, echoes, and birdsong, her nose bumped mine. It took a few attempts before it turned into a kiss.

"Oh! Oh, that," I said stupidly.

It was awkward afterwards, so we drifted around the park exploring the statues and talking of nothing much.

Eventually, we sat in a field of red flowers as tall as us. Our conversation inevitably led to the trial.

"We shouldn't even be friends," I said. "Our people fought in Craw war. My people killed yours."

"Because I'm Ansar, and you're Exer? Those things doesn't make it difficult for us. Being from different creeds doesn't cause war. It's people who do. You're the only person I've met who gets what it's like to be from Craw but can't remember it. Doesn't matter what creed you're from."

"I know, but..."

"Which faction are you? Isn't everyone from Craw either Perther or Fern?"

"Fern. At least, we used to be. Now, we're Exers. I've never known an Exer claim to be anything else."

Ren pulled me upright. "What a good way of looking at things! Exers are very wise. Time to visit your mermaids. It's what I meant about showing you something special. You're always wearing merfolk." She tugged the bracelet Korl had crafted for me into a long tail. "I knew you needed to see this."

"Have you seen the tunnel in Exer?"

"Yes! Many times. It's partly why the jealousy. I thought, I wish I lived there. Exer looks like the perfect home."

"I thought you despised me because I'm an Exer."

"Enough talk. Look, Devora."

She pulled me beyond a huge hedge. I looked up into a circle of twenty tall merfolk figurines facing one another. It was terrifying and magnificent. Imposing and otherworldly.

I covered my eyes with my hands and then peeped through my fingers. "Wow. I didn't expect this."

"I wanted you to see it, with me. I've not been the same since I first came. It reminded me of home, even though I don't remember Craw. I felt so homesick!"

I took my hand away and chanced a look at the stern figures and the distant Breen tower. Like guardians, they appraised the park and faraway places. Despite the circle, each stood alone.

Pink and purples tiles decorated the biggest. A merman

glittered with tiny torches. One mermaid had multicoloured lips and silver-streaked hair. Of all colours and sizes, some statues had happy expressions, others melancholy. At the base of each figurine, an open door beckoned and then led to rooms carved into the structures.

"This is where refugees escaped," Ren said. "The artist hid them and sealed up the doors. They transported them all the way through Mainland and went past the noses of soldiers and checkpoints. Nobody knew if the mermaids would be strong enough to survive the journey."

"So brave. I wish they were my family."

One figure had no face but a globe shape, instead, filled with nebulous colours and forms. I thought I saw fish and seals diving within the waters. Translucent material made up another, revealing a tiny baby within the womb.

One held my gaze longer than the rest. Rather than a mer form, writhing tentacles comprised the figure, with her head weighed down by seaweed. She didn't seem whole or complete and belonged neither to humankind or the ocean.

The statues silenced me. With all my heart, I wished my parents had been part of their creation, instead of drawn into hate and viciousness.

"I knew you'd like her," Ren said.

"Thank you for bringing me."

She kissed my cheek. "According to Ma, they represent the people and spirit of Craw. Behind the factions and war, there was always art and resilience. The war isn't the whole story. It won't last forever. We're part of these mermaids."

"They took away my citizenship. I'm not anything to do with Craw anymore. My brother says we're not Crawian now. Do you know why it's called Exer? Because we're ex-

Crawians." The words were difficult to utter.

"You'll always be Crawian."

"I'm not anything. I don't belong anywhere." I stood beneath the beast. "Like her. Don't you know Exers are children of monsters? The whole of Mainland wishes we didn't exist. They didn't kill us, but they wish we'd disappear."

"Rubbish. *I* don't wish so, nor do lots of people. Foreign armies don't get to wipe out your family lineage. Who are they anyway? A bunch of soldiers who don't even live here! All they did was make matters worse and then leave. You deserve to know where you come from and where your family went. It's your right."

"Deserve? Maybe we did unforgiveable things. Maybe I did." I waited three seconds. "I probably did."

"You were *three*. Humans aren't perfect, good creatures. We do amazing things—like make these mermaids—and terrible things. What matters now is what we do next and to keep trying."

"I still did those deeds."

Ren took my hand and looked up at the tentacles. "What's a monster anyway?"

"True. I don't know. I never liked the sweet mermaids in the tunnels. They get on my nerves! I only like the ones everyone else is scared of."

She laughed and hugged me. "Typical of you. I think you should wear a bracelet with the inscription *I like monsters*. Before the war, Arker's work was all around Breen. It's what I've heard. When the war was coming, she went into schools and gave children little mermaids so they didn't lose hope. Later on, they became symbols of resistance. I expect you know all this?"

"No. I don't think so," I said.

"Think. I've seen the tunnels—I'm sure you do."

With knees pulled up, I contemplated what she'd said. Korl crafted figurines long into the night. Everyone slept while he crept from door to door leaving mermaid gifts on doorsteps and window ledges.

"Maybe I do," I said slowly.

Every Exer visited the mermaid tunnels and had contributed to their birth and maintenance. Ren was right. Phantom tides and the essence of Craw culture was imbibed into us.

"I knew of her once," I continued. "The merfolk anyway. My cousin remembered her. My brother too. You're right! Her merfolk have inspired Exers. I don't suppose we had anyone else."

I couldn't fully explain our longing and loss. The tunnel was a substitute and record for families and homes, pride and culture. Over long years without elders or knowledge of how to love ourselves, we'd invented new festivals and marked the passing of time with Korl's figurines.

"My brother makes tiny mermaids and leaves them outside the children's flats. At festival times, he got all the kids to help him weave a huge tapestry. We hung it across the entrance to Exer."

"That's so lovely!"

"He—he has a gun and is the Exer gang leader. I think, maybe, he's killed people and lost hope. What if he leads the gangs into war?"

Ren tried to hide her shock. "But you don't know for sure?"

"No. He won't talk to me. Not enough. And I can't talk

to him. There's something between us. Sometimes I think I don't want to know."

"Maybe you're wrong? He could be scared. A lot of people have kept guns and weapons and never used them. My Da has a gun! The way we deal with fear is part of what's wrong with Mainland. You say your brother makes little mermaids? Doesn't sound like something a vicious gang leader would do."

"But it's true."

"Exactly what I'm saying. He makes mermaids *and* is gang leader. That's complex. He has a wish to make others happy, especially children. Not for his own glory or to be praised. Mostly people who do good deeds like others to know about it. His mermaids are wishes for things to be different."

"Maybe."

"Walk inside the circle. Maybe the mermaids will give you answers."

Ren moved away and let me walk alone inside the immense circle. Tentatively, I touched the tails and looked up into fiery eyes, almost expecting the stones to move and apprehend me for my boldness. I feared their wrath for the crimes committed in Craw. I feared their compassion. More than anything, I wanted to walk among them as equal kin and as a girl with ideas instead of bitterness and images of guns.

"I want to be like you," I whispered.

Within the commanding circle, my breath slowed and the clamminess on my forehead eased. "Give me a sign?" I soon reached the end of the circle and was back with the tall daisies and the wooden bench.

Ren said, with vast, frightened eyes, "Is he your brother? Jon Kraken?"

Under the watchful gaze of the merfolk there was no path but truth.

"Jon's my cousin. I love him so much." My voice sprang out, loud and clear as the birds above. "I have to go with him, to the speak-and-listen. I want—" I drew breath.

"Go on?" Ren said.

"To speak. To be with Jon and Korl, whatever happens. To let them know I stand with them, whatever they say. To accept the blame for what my family did. To hear what happened. To *move forward* from where we are. So many lives have been lost. Our own children are being born, and so isn't it time for change? My brother and I argue so much. He thinks I hate him, but I don't."

Ren almost spoke and then stopped herself. She brought out the orange stone from a pocket and placed it between our two palms.

"This is your stone. It will bring you the confidence to do whatever you were meant to. I know it's not as strong as what's inside you—but I don't think you do. Belief is stronger than any symbol."

She pressed, and I pressed back.

"You have to do it, Devora. Go with your brother and cousin. Be together at this trial that will tie the lost threads of your life. I've got the court application forms in my bag. Post them today; or there won't be time."

"Okay."

In the circle of mermaids, we completed the basic information and only paused at the section asking for names. I noticed a butterfly resting on Ren's dress and wrote Korl's name. I heard lyrical birdsong and added Anees.

"I don't know what Jon's going to say or why he went. I don't remember anything. Only wisps of dreams. I think it was bad. I guess you understand—you've read the books!"

"Whatever it is, it's not going to kill you," Ren said, offering me a massive apple. "The truth can hurt, but it can't be worse than not knowing. The speak-and-listen won't change what happened, but it could make the future better." She hesitated. "Some of it might be from books. But—you get the gist?"

"How do you know?" I bit, apple juice escaping onto my chin.

"Because your cousin wouldn't have left if he believed so," she said easily. "He's gone because he had to. And your brother loves you. Otherwise, he wouldn't have cared for you so well all these years. You don't seem like a girl who hasn't been loved. You're brave enough to be defiant and angry. You've got the biggest attitude I've ever seen!"

"What do I say, when I can't remember? How can I speak for Jon and Korl?" I named the dread which kept me from sleeping.

She shrugged as though the answer was simple. "Speak—and listen! You can do it. Talk about your family and all the things you've done together. It's obvious how close you are. Devora, you're a strong person. I knew it when you asked the teacher about the trials. Did you see how astonished she was? It was such a big question! I thought— she's brave. A girl like that can make things happen. Not lawyers and politicians. What do they know?"

I didn't feel big or capable. In another great gush of emotion, I cried, and she held me.

"You have to go. Even if it's very difficult. Otherwise, you'll always regret it. Your cousin has given you this precious chance."

"What if we killed your relatives?" The words blasted free, harsh and raw. "What if *I* did?"

"You didn't. We got out in time."

"Ansars. Your kind and your people. I might have done!"

She didn't loosen or let go of my hands. "I don't know. How can I say? What can we do about it? Nothing. About asking someone to speak—you have to listen and accept what they say. Isn't it the purpose of the trials? Things happened to us, but it doesn't mean they have to keep on ruining lives. Ansars, Perthers, Ferns. *We're* born of those creeds. If *we* can't be big enough to start again, then who?"

We talked until the sun began to fade and the birds formed long lines above.

As we walked back past the stone lions, Ren asked, "What do you wish could happen at the speak-and-listen? What would the best outcome be for you?"

I didn't want to say, "For Korl to stop killing and never to see blood again." Ren wasn't ready to hear such things. Yet I was drunk from the statues and the possibilities. When my answer came, it was honest.

"To live in a better place with my brother and Jon and for Exers to understand they exist and are valid and wanted. To know there's a future? There're no words to apologise for what happened in Craw. But if we could—talk about it? Learn from it. Not allow more lives to be ruined, and not to sit back and hope someone else will sort it out. To know *we* can do it."

"Imagine if you did all this—what else would you want? I mean, for you? What do *you* want, Devora?"

I staggered from the hugeness of the question. For a long time, I considered possibilities and realities.

"To not have this *thing* inside anymore." I pressed my chest. "Guilt. Questions. The toxic space between me and Korl. To know *how* to think about my parents. I wish I knew how."

Ren put a hand up to her face. "Oh."

Together, we watched the sun go down. The afternoon came to an end, and we walked away from the park in the evening sunshine.

"Time to say goodbye. Post the application here. We have the power of the mermaids behind us," Ren said. "There's something I have to tell you."

I slotted the application through the postal hole while she hugged me from behind. "What is it?"

"When the teacher told us about an Exer joining the class, I was terrified. There are rumours about Exers biting people and carrying knives. I thought you might be similar. I told Ma, and she said the best thing was to make friends with you. She asked how I'd like it if people spread gossip about me?"

She stopped for breath. I wasn't worried or surprised by anything said so far.

"I didn't like you either," I said. "I thought you were rich and spoiled. Every time you talked about Craw, I could have slapped you. What changed your mind?"

"I forgot you were an Exer and started thinking of you as Devora. I noticed the hairs on your earlobes and the scar on your wrist. One day, you wore socks with crabs on!"

"That's bad. My girlfriend only kissed me to please her mother."

"Don't forget the crab socks."

Shield Diary Six
Korl

It's been weeks. Uncle hasn't been back. Good flipping riddance. Jon's getting better. I'm going to get us out, like Ma said. I keep thinking about it. I don't care what it takes. I'm going to get Devi, Jon, and me out of here. I'm trying not to think about the little kids, the other shields, because I don't know if I can leave them behind.

I've got a plan.

I'm going to get us out.

Me. I'm Korl Kraken, and I'm going to get us out.

We've got a plan!

"Shh," I tell the shields. "Don't move. Not even a muscle. Wait until I give the signal. What's the signal?"

"Raise your hand," Oosha says. "Right up in the air!"

"Right. Very good! When I raise my hand—what do you do?" I ask in my teacher voice.

"We run out of the door, into the big light of victory," Nila says. "We jump over the body of the major. If there's blood, we won't look."

"Well, yeah, we run out of the doors, yeah. I dunno if the big light of victory is going to be there. One step at a time. We run out of the doors, and we keep on running."

"Where to? Is it to our ma's?" Heva asks.

Oh, gods. Their mas. This is where the plan falls apart. What plan could work when there are missing mas and das? "Just follow me."

Jon won't speak, not a word. All he does is smile at Devi's songs. I've started making a new book, a kind of alphabet. I'm Korl, and I'm going to get us out of here. First, I'm going to help Jon speak. Not with words, because he's used them all up. No words left. I'm going to help Jon speak by using the mermaid book. It doesn't matter if all the words have gone because there are always merfolk. It's what Arker Fi taught me, and I won't ever forget.

Yesterday, I asked the stone mermaid for help, and she told me, "Do it. Make the book and get them out."

I made the book. Jon points at the letters, and I translate what he's saying. It gives us something to do.

Devi says, "Draw me a mermaid apple," so I do it. We write *apple* on the paper. Jon smiles and smiles, and my heart breaks into tiny bits of angry shields.

When the door rattles, I'm going to be ready. I'm going to get us out. Like the mermaid says.

Chapter Fourteen

AFTER THE BUTTERFLIES and birds of Berker Park, the dullness of our home was all too apparent. There were damp patches in the corners and the ever-present smell of mould. I hoped, for Jon's sake, he never came back.

However, giggles bubbled from the direction of the kitchen, and I peeped in to find Anees and Korl cuddled up together.

"Hello," I called.

"Where've you been?"

Almost guiltily Korl slid his arm away. I wanted to explain that I knew about their relationship and welcomed it. Broaching any serious topic seemed increasingly impossible, so I chose an easier subject of conversation.

The afternoon I had spent with Ren was fresh in my

mind, and I considered how to tell Korl about the park without getting into trouble. "Why are you inside? It's hot. I went somewhere nice."

"Where could we go?" Anees said.

"There's a park about two miles away. It's right between Exer and Breen."

"Berker," Korl interrupted. "You mean Berker Park?"

It hadn't occurred to me he would already know about the mermaids. "Yes! How do you know about it?"

"I've been hundreds of times." He looked towards Anees. "I'll take you. Do you want to go?"

"Did you see the merfolk?" she asked. "Did you stand inside?"

"Yeah! I—" My brother stopped, looked down, and rubbed at the table with one finger.

"What?" Anees said. "Aren't you going to tell us? You can't stop now."

He kissed her forehead. "Nothing much. I've seen the merfolk statues. I'll take you both. It's like stepping back in time to Craw, and at the same time, it's like nothing you've ever seen before. The first time I went, I cried."

The uncomfortable atmosphere dissipated. My brother's open admission was startling, but Anees only murmured and kissed his cheeks as if she weren't surprised.

"What did you do at school today? What laws did you study?" My brother met my eyes and then winked to let me know I was forgiven for lying about my course. Or maybe he'd always known, and paranoia had tricked me into hurtful assumptions.

"The teacher didn't show, so I went to Berker Park instead with my friend. Did you know the artist is from Craw?"

I held my breath and waited to see if he'd interrogate me about Ren.

"Arker Fi is the mermaid gatekeeper of Craw," he said. "She used to come into our schools. You've met her, Devi, though you were only tiny. She gave the kids mermaids and told us never to forget where we came from. I want the Exer kids to have the same." My brother's face softened. "I'm thrilled you've seen them. I don't know why I didn't take you before; it's your history as much as mine."

I held my breath at the magnitude of his statement and couldn't meet his eyes in case I cried with relief.

"Because you're only now seeing what's possible." Anees traced his ear with one long finger. "We have to say yes to more things, remember?"

"I know, and I want to. I do want so much more for us," he said softly.

It seemed we had come far since the night Jon left. My cousin used to say Korl had been much more damaged by war than me. Still, it was unsettling and raw to witness the transformation. It was me who changed the subject and who wasn't ready.

"Shall I cook?"

"We'll do it together. Anything." My brother rubbed his stomach. "I'm starving."

"Even for *my* cooking? Who's coming tonight?" I opened the fridge and began taking out food.

"Just us. I've sent the others away."

It had been days since the gang had called by. That, too, was a new development. I wondered if the others would resent his intimacy with Anees or be glad to be free of the Krakens.

"Can I help, Devi?" Anees leaned across and kissed his cheek quickly. "Then we can talk about Craw and the trials. And no silliness from you, grumpy bear."

My brother laughed and rubbed his hair ruefully, and then went back to drawing. "Fair enough. Suppose it's time. I've messed around for long enough, haven't I?"

The shock must have shown because Anees winked at me and smothered a laugh.

When my brother disappeared into his room to get more pencils, I said under my breath, "Grumpy bear? Oh, you're good! Much better than me."

"He's talking about the trial. All the time, like he can't stop. *Could* we get away from here? Permanently, I mean. I don't see how we could ever come back. You know if we stay, it's only a matter of time? Farlo's in deep. He's going to drag Korl down with him."

I processed the information with some bitterness. There was much Jon, and maybe Korl, had protected me from knowing.

"No more blood though. Please?" I said. "There's got to be another way. Mix the flour for flatbreads?"

"I agree. If we're starting somewhere else, it has to be a fresh start. Not bad memories or secrets." Anees poured water into the pan and lit the oven. "I love doing this stuff." She sighed. "Cooking and talking with nothing hanging over us. Don't you think Korl looks better?"

"Yeah. How come you're not working tonight?"

Jon used to say the gangs were a way of socialising and communicating, and when Exers arrived in Breen, gangs had replaced families.

"Sick of the infighting," Anees said. "Things have

become worse over the last few months. Only Korl keeps the peace. It won't ever end. It'll go on and on. I want *more*. So much more." She mouthed around her hands. "If Korl leaves for the trials, I don't know what will happen to Exer."

I'd not considered my brother as protector of the peace. "What do *you* want, Anees?"

She answered without hesitation. "To be me. Somewhere I can walk freely and hold my partner's hand. Where people think about one another and animals because they want to. Because it's the only way. No more greed or me-me-me."

"Do you believe we could get to Craw?" I said breathlessly.

"Yes! We could *do it*. I've seen the way he looks when he talks about the speak-and-listen. It's reminded him of Craw and of what we left behind."

"I can't tell what he thinks," I said.

"You're the last person he'd talk to."

"Me? Why?"

Hurt must have shown on my face, and she put an arm protectively around my shoulders. "Because you're his little sister. He wants to protect you is all."

"He won't tell me a thing about my parents. Or Jon. If Korl loves me—he'd see how going to the speak-and-listen is a good thing."

"Devora, you can be very slow for someone who wants to study law! Think about it. Think hard and deep. Have you never heard rumours? What's the thing Korl is most afraid of?"

"Being locked up?" It was a guess. The recent hot topics of gossip were centred upon gangs, guns, and fights.

"He's terrified for *you*. Not for himself, or Jon. Or, maybe so, but mostly for you and the other younger Exers. Because you don't remember what happened. We do. We already know. It's why he won't talk. Because he doesn't want you to carry the things he knows. Devi—I remember what I did. Trust me, I wish I didn't."

Her green eyes locked with mine. I wanted to protest in the way Ren would have done and remind Anees she was only a child doing what she was told.

The pain in her eyes stopped me, and I hugged her instead. "Why doesn't he just tell me everything?"

She run a hand through her hair. "Haven't you heard people talk? Think, Devi. I'm not going to be the one to tell you."

I remembered what Farlo said the night at the field and again in the kitchen. "I don't know. Something about guns? Tell me," I whispered.

She mouthed *Jon's father*.

I couldn't recall anything and shook my head. "I don't know. Jon never said anything, and neither has anyone else. I don't even know his parents' names."

"He was leader of the Fern army. A politician intending to lead the city into a position of strength by suppressing other creeds, especially Ansars. Many Mainlanders followed him and his vision of supremacy. Rumour has it *Korl* killed him. One of his own kin."

I covered my mouth with my hands. No Crawian would ever kill one of their own family.

"How? Korl was only a kid. I don't believe it. I'd have heard about it by now. And anyway, it sounds as if he was more than a piece of work."

If it was true, then Korl might not be welcomed back to Exer City. If Craw refused to return his citizenship, he'd have nowhere to go. Once the knowledge was made public, his life would be in jeopardy.

She pulled a face. "It's only what I've guessed and might not be true. Who knows what really happened? Maybe nobody."

"Shitting hell."

"Don't swear. Jon didn't like it, nor do I." She swatted me with a cloth. "We can't stop the process anyway. It's too late. Breeners came here last night again looking for a fight. Word has got out about the speak-and-listen and made people uncertain and angry."

"Because Farlo incites them! Maybe we should stay here and sort it out after all? Exer is our city," I said slowly.

"We have to try for more. Not only for us but for all of Exer. And have faith—because Jon's clever. He wouldn't have taken such a risk if he thought there was no chance it would end well. He loves you and Korl more than his own life."

"True. I miss him."

Anees gripped my hand. "Don't look so tragic. I still think the trials are the right thing to do."

Right then, my brother returned. When I stirred too vigorously, the wooden spoon clattered across the floor.

"What's up with you, Devi Bee? You look like you've swallowed a whale," he said.

"Nothing. It's *Devora* Bee, not Devi. When are you going to learn? I'm not a little tiny bee, thank you very much! I'm *Devora*."

"Okay, okay. Don't shout. What have you two been

talking about?" My brother kissed Anees's palm and slid his arms around her waist. "It's very cosy in here."

They kissed. It was fascinating how they constantly reached and checked for each other. Only a few weeks ago, such public affection didn't seem possible.

"We need to talk about how we're going to get to Craw, Korli, and where we'll stay," Anees said.

I hooted uncharitably. "I've already posted the application forms—for—for school. It was part of my course. We should receive tickets for the three of us. The wheels are turning. *Korli.*"

My brother's handsome face remained impassive. "No, Devi. It wasn't for school. If we're doing this, then no more lies. You're way old enough for the truth, little sis."

My first instinct was to lie because it was easier and less painful. After thinking of the mermaids in the park, I told the truth.

"Okay. It wasn't for school, no. It was for us. For Jon, and you. For me, and Anees. I guess for all the Exers."

"Good! As long as you understand what it's going to mean and what you're going to hear at the speak-and-listen. I might not be able to protect you. Do you see?"

For an instant, he looked desperate and devastated. I scratched at a hole in the table and didn't know what to say.

"I don't know what I'm going to hear because I'm not a mind reader. How could I? I want to help Jon."

Korl abruptly stood, and the chair scraped on jagged tiles. Involuntarily I jumped back and knocked over a cold cup of coffee.

"Sorry." I mopped the liquid up quickly.

After a pause, he said, "All right. I've made a decision.

We'll go to the speak-and-listen. We can get trains. I don't know how we'll pay for the tickets, but I'll think of something." He turned to Anees and cradled her face in his hands.

"You're right. It's time to make a stand. We can't live like this. I don't want my little sister to lie to me." His voice caught. "I'm sorry, Devi. How did we get so far from who we are?"

"I don't know," I said honestly.

Anees flung her arms around my brother and covered his face with kisses.

"I've posted application forms too," my brother said. "I don't know why you're so excited, darling. From what I remember, Craw is even colder than Breen." And he kissed her on the nose.

I DREAMT OF gunshots and awoke suddenly to hear low voices. My brother often held midnight meetings, so it wasn't unusual. The dream lingered.

I felt sure he was up to no good and crept from my bed to listen. When the front door closed, I scrambled into some clothes and stepped out into the dark streets of Exer.

Two figures walked stealthily in the direction of the woods. I stayed back like the previous time and kept in the shadows. When they reached the junction between Exer and the wilderness, my brother stopped and placed what looked like a large bag on the ground. I assumed it was filled with weapons.

My heart beat fast, and rage erupted like fire. I mentally called him all the names in Mainland. There was no doubt he'd lied to me and Anees and had no intention of changing direction or going to the trials.

They picked up the bag and, instead of heading into the woods, turned sharply onto another street. I sped up and ran silently to the corner, making sure to crouch low behind vehicles so they wouldn't see me. When the figure loomed from behind me, I screamed loudly and kicked out.

"Shut up!" A hand covered my mouth. Someone pulled me into a deserted alleyway and thrust me against the wall.

I struggled and fought the person as my brother had taught me. "Get off me! It's Devora Kraken. If my brother finds out you've touched me—!"

The figure peeled away their head covering to reveal Anees. "Devi! What the hell are you doing here? I thought you were going to jump us."

My brother appeared seconds later with the bag. When he saw it was me, he chuckled and dropped the bag onto the ground. "Devi!"

"Your sister has quite a knack for following us," Anees said.

I gulped and waited for what I knew would be an almighty ticking off. After the night in the woods, my brother had made me swear I'd never follow him again.

"I thought you were, um, burglars," I said.

Instead of shouting, they began necking and seemed to forget about me altogether.

I watched for a while and then poked my brother with my shoe. "Would you stop! You lied to me. You're a stupid turnip head."

They ignored me. Furious and defiant, I bent and unzipped the bag. Fully expecting to find guns and knives, I couldn't have been more surprised to find perfectly painted and decorated mini-mermaids.

Eventually, my brother stopped his kissing and remembered I was supposed to be grounded. "Hey! Remember when I said not to follow me or leave the flat at night?"

"I thought you were off killing. I was only trying to save your soul," I said.

"Killing?" He shook his head sadly and tried to tickle me under the chin. "When are you going to have faith in me? Even a little bit?"

Anees yawned and hoisted up the bag. "She can help. Grab a handle, Devi."

We walked the streets of Exer and the outskirts of Breen carrying poxy mermaids. My brother made me leave the stupid things on doorsteps with a card saying, *Look to the skies.* Worse, he insisted I kept copious notes of which gardens bore signs of children.

"I want to go *home.* I don't care which mermaid. I could break all their ugly necks," I said, often.

My brother had no sympathy. "Tough. You're here now. Pick a mermaid and quit moaning."

By the time we finished, dawn was breaking. I all but staggered back to the flat and collapsed into bed fully clothed.

Shield Diary Seven
Korl

We're ready! Have practised a thousand times. The plan is going to be engraved into my brain for the rest of my life. If I have one.

"Drill practice. Go!"

When I raise my hand, the kids sit silently, backs against the walls, knees up. I swear, for such young kids, they're surprisingly easy to train. One day, I'm going to go into schools, like Arker Fi, and teach kids how to draw mermaids. I'll help her carve the sculptures and tell the kids they can do anything, just like she did. I'll make up for what I'm about to do and only do good in the world. I'll never argue with people because they're from a different part of the city to me, and I won't ever, *ever*, use kids in wars.

When Uncle opens the door, I'll use my shield and bash him over the head. Not to protect his stupid army but to protect *us*. A shield's job is to stop death, and that's what I'm doing. I'm going to give him a chance to live. Though I loathe him, he's still Jon's da. I don't want my cousin hating me for the rest of our lives. If we get them.

When he falls to the floor, the kids will jump up and run out through the door, away into freedom. I'll tie Uncle up. The rope's ready and coiled around my waist. I've practised and practised. I'll tie his hands behind his back. Attach him to the kitchen door. Ignore all pleas and threats. Gag if necessary. When he's tied safely, me, Jon, and Devi will leave the Gatehouse.

It's going to be difficult walking away from the stone mermaid, but she says it's the right thing to do. If the kids have waited, we'll go together, holding hands. I can't make plans about where we'll go.

Ready. We're ready. It's taken ages to convince Jon, but finally, he finds the right page, the one with the smiling mermaid who looks like she's drunk.

CHAPTER FIFTEEN

THE TENSION BUILT, and Korl and I argued like hormonal beach crabs. Every night, we went out with a new bag of mermaids and returned home only once they'd all been distributed. He was ruthless about hitting targets and ensuring no child was left out.

"I'm *tired*. I don't want to do any more. Isn't it enough I have to seal the stupid things? You can't make me do more. It's not ethical. I'm going to report you to the authorities."

My brother snorted and tugged my earlobe. "Not ethical! Try to see the bigger picture, Devi—the children need this glimmer of hope. It's all I can leave them with when we go to Craw."

"Turnip head," I replied.

"Very mature! And stop swearing."

I constantly checked for letters. We didn't have a letter box or ordinarily receive mail other than bills, so we didn't know what to expect.

When it arrived, the white envelope had been pushed underneath the door. It looked official and bore a seal in the shape of a shield.

I shouted loud enough to be heard in Craw. "It's here!"

My brother rushed from the kitchen where he'd been drinking coffee and stared down at my hand. When I tried to make him take the envelope, he shook his head.

"Open it!" I shouted.

"You open it. I'll jinx it."

"Shut up," I retorted and ripped open the letter.

"Well? What does it say?" Korl clutched at Anees as if she were a cushion. "I'm sure it'll be a rejection."

"Yeah," she muttered.

They huddled together in the dark corridor until I read aloud:

"We are delighted to receive your application to attend the speak-and-listen. You are invited to speak for Jon Kraken. During your stay, you are granted unlimited access to Craw, provided you follow guidelines and do not go into restricted zones. Accommodation and meals will be paid for and provided by the state of Craw."

I waited for cheers that didn't come. "Well? What are you standing there for? Will anyone speak?"

My brother sniffed. "*Delighted.* Very pompous."

"They've said yes?" Anees asked carefully. "Did I hear right? Is it yes?"

In a muddle of arms, they grabbed at each other in the early morning sunshine, and the tension gripping us for weeks was released. Korl whooped and chased me, and I felt happier than I had for ages.

"Have you told the gangs we're leaving for the speak-and-listen?" Anees asked.

During the week, she'd ended the pretence and moved into Korl's room with a few bags and a box. Bersha and Tomi had said nothing, only watched with curious eyes. Farlo slammed doors and snapped at everyone.

"Yes," Korl said.

"You *told* them?" I spluttered.

"Of course. Exers are my people. Our people. When word got around that Jon had left for the trials, it caused more fighting than ever. Fear, I guess. I don't know how the gangs will handle it when I've gone too. I hope they'll wait for my word before they do anything—but I can't guarantee it. Tomi will wait for my sign. I've told him he has my blessing to join the Turner family till then."

"Yeah. He'll be okay there," Anees said. "Bersha too. The Turners are okay."

Gang members shifted alliances often. If it didn't mean losing face, Korl normally agreed to such a change.

"What are we going to tell Farlo? He'll make trouble, and he's not like lovely Tomi," I pointed out.

"I've already told him," Korl said. "Maybe he'll be happy to see us go and wish us luck?"

Anees said nothing, but I could tell she wanted to. When Korl went to the bathroom, she grabbed my elbow and hissed in my ear. "It was Farlo who caused the blood the night Jon left."

"What? Why?"

"To force Jon to leave? Or to force Korl into taking up

arms? Serious stuff. There can't be a happy ending. Farlo's been trying it on for ages. Did you know he started the riots in Breen? He's vindictive and won't stop until he brings about war. He hates to see Korl happy and able to see a way out. I don't know why Korl doesn't see what a threat he is!"

"I *told* Korl Farlo was planning behind his back, and he didn't do anything! If that rat gets wind we're going to leave, he might do something drastic."

"Korl will look after it. Nobody knows the gangs like he does. He wants the best for every Exer. I think, maybe, the gangs might well follow him to Craw. After all, he's leader. They love him."

I tutted. "He couldn't lead an army of ants."

She leaned across and tweaked my ear. "Trust your brother. One day, you will."

Shield Diary Eight
Korl

Uncle doesn't come. Nobody comes. The bombs are loud. The kids are wearing ear muffs. Nobody speaks anymore. Except me. I can't stop talking. Words come out like air. I don't even care that I get no answers. I don't care.

"Jon. Where do you think he is?"

No answer.

"Devi. Drink your water."

No reply. She's drawing mermaids.

"Arlo. Yeah, you can be my lieutenant, sure. You're in our family. You can be—The Watch. Okay?"

"Can I?" Arlo-Farlo is the only kid who answers. He's kind of cute and keeps me company. "I won't leave you. You can rely on me."

We try kicking our way out of the door. We don't succeed. Jon and I work on the mermaid book. It's weird how actual words don't say as much as they used to. I think about all the words the world wasted and how it turned into this gigantic war which locked us in a stone gatehouse.

Me and Jon have whole conversations without speaking; Devi too. Sometimes, hours pass with the only sound my pencils on paper.

"What happened out there?" I ask Jon all the time, even though it makes him huddle up like a hedgehog. "What's going on?"

One time, he doesn't huddle and cry. He flits through the book. It's how I got to draw dead mermaids. I wouldn't let Devi look. Mermaids are lame, but even I got sad. My cousin did that for us, so we didn't have to.

It made me more determined. I'm Korl Kraken. I'm going to get us out. Save Jon so he won't ever have to do their dirty work again. I'll get a job and keep us fed and safe and warm. Whatever it takes, I'm going to do it. I'll make sure we forget about this shit and have a brilliant life. Any life.

I hug Jon until he stops crying. "It wasn't your fault."

My cousin used to come fishing with me. Now, we draw pictures of dead mermaids.

Another day goes past. Uncle doesn't come. Nobody comes.

"Wait," says the stone mermaid.

CHAPTER SIXTEEN

AT THE OUTSKIRTS of the city, the acrid smell of burning was overpowering. Severely panicked, I ran towards school. Within days, the city had become unrecognisable. Rather than bright baskets of flowers, litter and empty beer bottles covered the pavements. Cafés were shuttered with padlocks, and even the twenty-four-hour shop Eileen used regularly was closed. What had been a busy hub was now a ghost town.

The speed with which the city had shut down proved it wasn't the first time the people had known war. I remembered what Eileen had said about Perther unrest.

By the time I reached school, I was sweaty, out of breath, and sure it was too late. Will ran across from the office carrying piles of fire extinguishers, and I could have wept with relief. It didn't seem possible I'd known him only a few months. In that time, he and Eileen had become a part of my life.

"Are you all right?" he asked me. "You shouldn't be out alone. It's not safe, especially for Exers."

"I'm fine. Don't exaggerate."

He dropped the books and drew me into the office. "You're going to Craw, yes? You need to leave, Devi. Don't wait any longer, or you might not get there. For now, the trouble is here, but who knows how long before it reaches Exer?"

I caught my breath. Looking around the familiar office with its tiny sculptures of dolphins, I wished I didn't have to leave.

"Feels like you only started yesterday. What are we going to do without you?" Will echoed my thoughts.

"I don't want to go. All these years and suddenly I found somewhere I like and now we have to leave. It's so typical of Exer luck."

"But you're going home. The speak-and-listen is only the start of something better. For us all." Will picked up my bag and traced the outline of a mermaid riding a wave. My brother had made the patch from coarse blue cloth and sewn it onto my bag the night before I started school. "Who made this?"

"My brother. He's very clever with sewing. At lots of things, really."

"I knew it! On the day we met, I saw this on your bag. And that." He found a whale fob, and another depicting a puffer fish. "I knew you were my kind and you'd do amazing things. Your family too. It's written all over your face, and it's in your bones. Skarles know stuff. You're of the sea. The tides and the fish are pulling you back. Your brother, too, if the patch is anything to go by. He's leaving you clues, you see. He might not know it, but it's what they are."

"Oh," I said, noticing the vast number of sea items about my person. As well as my bag, I wore a top with a wave print. "Maybe."

Then I remembered all the silly items I'd made for Korl over the last few weeks—a lizard made from reeds, the mashed potato shaped into a whale.

"A person can leave the sea, but it won't ever leave you. You know I'm right," Will said.

I wondered how I'd be able to say goodbye. Other than the Krakens and Ren, Will and Eileen were the only friends I'd ever made.

"I don't know much about the sea," I said. "I've read about the history of Craw. I wish I knew more."

Will reached across and handed me a small box. "Soon you will. This is for you. Don't open it until you get home. We'll both be embarrassed, and it's not good for my reputation as a scary guard."

I took the box awkwardly and wished I'd thought to bring something to say goodbye. "I don't know what to say. What is it? You didn't have to buy me anything."

"Nothing much. Eileen and I—we've waited for this for a long, long time. For the speak-and-listen, and someone like you. For what will come after. We always knew there'd come a time when Mainland would be ready. When we can return to Craw because it's been too long. Have you ever started a Monday knowing it's going to be a really tiring week?"

"Yeah," I said. The week after Jon left was the hardest week of my life.

"It's what it's been like since the Craw wars. One bottomless well of a week. You keep falling and falling. Sometimes you think your foot has snagged on the side and you're going to reach the end. Then you accept the descent and stop hoping to reach the bottom."

He wrapped his arms around his waist.

I wiped my eyes. "I have to go and find Ren. How will I say goodbye?"

"You won't have to because she's gone to Craw too. She told us yesterday." He reached into his pocket and withdrew something wrapped in crinkled tissue. "She asked me to give you this. Her family had to leave sooner than planned."

"What? Why?"

"Now don't get panicky," Will said. "Breathe. Ren's safe. Her building was set on fire yesterday. The last twenty-four hours have been chaos. People want to talk, but first, they want to shout and draw attention. It will die down when the speak-and-listen begins."

"I'll never see her again."

"Trust she'll find you. I promise. Ansars do what they say they will. Now go before the doors are sealed. Shall I walk you home?"

"No. I'll be fine."

He gripped my shoulders and touched my forehead lightly with his. "This is the Skarle shake of goodbye. Not a forever kind of goodbye."

He took my hand and wiggled my little finger with his own.

"We'll speak again, Devora of the sea. Me and Eileen

will be waiting to hear from you. Don't forget us. Ours has been a short connection, but it runs deep. When you're settled, send us your address. One day, we'll surf together!"

"Tell Eileen goodbye. I'm so sorry I missed her," I said heavily.

The front doors banged suddenly. A crowd appeared and blocked the entrance. Some people bore torches, and others held up what looked like weapons.

"Too late! Wear this. I'm taking you home." Will thrust a helmet my way and pulled me towards another exit where a motorbike and carriage leaned against the wall.

"Hold on tight," he said.

I pulled on the helmet and clambered on. I wrapped my arms around his stout figure and held on for my life. The speed of the bike matched my racing heart and fear of what the future would bring. We sped past crowds and chaos and wound through deserted streets and back roads until Breen was behind us.

"Almost there," Will called.

We passed Berker Park, and I bid a silent farewell to the stone merfolk. Soon we reached the woods bordering Exer. My heart sank when I saw the gangs. The trouble was about to reach my home and family.

I shouted to Will. "Turn left. They'll knock us off. Take the forest route."

As we swerved, I got a good look at the person in front—Farlo. Anees had been right all along. If he reached Korl, I feared he would force my brother into joining the riot.

Will shouted above the roar of the engine. "Where to?"

"The last block! The one with the red merboy mural."

We parked and hurried inside, where my brother and

Anees waited. The kitchen had been cleaned and everything piled up. At the side of the kitchen table, the mermaid box was empty but for one little statue.

Korl pulled me into a hug that threatened to squeeze out all the air.

"Thank gods you're back. We need to leave. I've said my goodbyes to the gangs, and left instructions. I don't know if they'll listen."

Will took off his helmet and held out a hand. "I'm your friend, Will Bossu. It's time to go to the train station, but it's too dangerous to leave from Breen. I can take you into Enu instead. Let's go now."

I looked questioningly from the empty box to my brother.

"Every child. I didn't leave anyone out." Korl took out the last doll and offered it to Will. "Do you need hope? Look to the sea and the skies. I promise I'll do what I can. She will rise!"

Will grinned and accepted the mermaid gracefully. "I know it. Thank you. I'll keep her safe until we meet again. I'll be watching the skies for your sign."

We left Exer City with nothing but a few bags, the mermaid book, and my parcels. Anees locked up the flat and slipped the key under the shark rock by the door. We walked away from the place we had called home for fifteen years with only a cursory backwards glance.

"Funny. I thought I'd feel sad," Anees murmured, echoing the thoughtful expression on my brother's face.

At the station, Will saw us onto the train. His waving figure, tall as a volcano, was the last thing I saw as we sped away.

Part Two

See you a monster,

Crawling from the sea?

Hear only sorrow,

For all that cannot be?

Or see you such beauty

Of an outstretched hand?

And endless sweet tomorrows

Dancing on the sand?

Shield Diary Nine
Korl

The door.
We're ready.
I'm up.
Arm high.
The kids move like wind, squashing their backs against the wall like we practised.
Legs apart. Shield in hand. I'm ready.
We're ready.
I'm Korl Kraken, and I'm going to get us out.
The door opens.
Uncle staggers in.
Drunk.
Gun in hand.
"Time to move! Stand outside in a line!" Uncle shouts.
I don't move. My shield falls to the floor.
The kids don't move.
Devi doesn't move.

"Wait," the stone mermaid says.

Silence, the biggest, loudest silence in the whole world, and the universe becomes a freezing block that holds me until the end of time.

"Move it! Time to fight! What did you think the training was for?" Uncle shouts.

I don't move.

The kids watch me.

We don't move.

The kids don't move.

I'm on the floor.

The creeps.

I don't move.

"Wait," says the stone mermaid.

"Please, Uncle. Don't make us go out there. Please?" I say.

"Give him one chance," the stone mermaid says.

"Please? Please let us go, Uncle? Let us go. Unlock the gateway, and let us go. Please?"

"Get up off the floor," my uncle shouts and reaches for his gun. "Krakens do not beg."

I don't move.

The kids don't move because I told them to wait for the signal.

Uncle slides to the floor, drunk. His gun clatters and rolls.

Devi moves.

Takes the gun.

Takes the gun.

Takes the gun.

After the explosion, Jon takes the gun from Devi's little

hand. "Devi Bee. I shot him. It was an accident. Not you? When you're older, I want you to remember me saying this. Do you hear me? It was *me*."

He picks Devi up and kisses her again and again. I throw up. I'm shaking and I can't stop.

"Korl Kraken! Leave," says the stone mermaid. "Go now. Take the children. Leave no one behind. I'll wait for you. Go now."

Jon hugs me until the voice stops. "It's time to go. Can't you hear the stone mermaid telling us to go?"

He holds my hand, and we walk outside.

The kids are waiting for us in silence, blinking at the light and the sun.

"Sorry. I'm so sorry. I love you," I tell Jon. If I never say any more words, I want these to be my last words.

He smiles, and it's almost the same as when we used to go fishing. "I love you too. And Devi. Sorry for what? Kids aren't shields, or guns, or knives. Kids are kids."

I think of Ma and how she used to bring me breakfast in bed. I remember what she said. "We have to go the other way. Back inside. Get Uncle's keys and unlock the Gate-house."

"What? But the Army. No. Let's go into Craw. Time for us to fight back!" Farlo says.

I look at my cousin. "What shall we do?" I can't be in charge anymore. I can't take these kids into Craw to fire guns. I can't do it. I love these kids.

"Crawians never betray their own," Arlo says. "No surrender."

"Across the bridge," says the stone mermaid. "Run! Run!"

Nobody speaks. We hold hands and make a snake. Jon at the front, limping, Devi next, clutching the mermaid book and her doll. The kids. Me, last.

We go back into the Gatehouse.

We stop and look at the body of my uncle. The kids start crying. The snake falls apart.

"I can't," Jon says. "I can't touch him."

It's Arlo who gets the keys. He sits, puts his hand into Uncle's pocket, and gets the keys. "Here, Korl. Tell us what to do."

"Form the line again," I say.

Jon leads with keys in his hand. We walk through the Gatehouse, right to the stone doors. "Are you sure?" he says.

"Get them out, Korl Kraken," the stone mermaid says. "Run! Run!"

After this, I can't make another decision. Whatever the army does, at least someone else will be making the decisions.

"Do it, Jon," I say.

Jon unlocks the Gatehouse.

CHAPTER SEVENTEEN

THE TRAIN JOURNEY passed with joy and laughter. My brother relaxed and talked with me like he used to years before.

"I didn't think we'd get here and couldn't dare imagine. I'm sorry it took so long. I was wrong about a lot of things, and I was weak. I doubted myself and my history."

Before, such words might have caused tears and helplessness. Now, I accepted he didn't have all the answers.

"Jon left because of me, didn't he?" I asked. "Because of that night. He saw me holding the gun, and it reminded him of another time. You can tell me about it now. I can take it."

"You can ask him. Just wait a little while longer?"

He brushed my hair and taught us how to make fishes from paper and played endless card games.

I enjoyed the attention and returned his kindness as best I could. "Are *you* all right? How are your hands?"

"My hands will recover. I'm not sure about the rest."

When he grew quiet, I left him alone. We looked with interest at the lands outside the window and then slept. Hours ticked by. Anees and I bought food and drinks from a kiosk on board and marvelled at the selection of sweets.

When my brother was refreshed, I tackled him again. "So, what's the rest? *Tell* me."

Without hesitation, he spoke. "I'm not all right, no. Terrified we've left our home again. Worried I've left Exer City. If war comes—what will happen to the children of Exer? To Tomi, Farlo, and Bersha? To our neighbours and friends? Will they wait for my word, or will they fight mindlessly?"

He gulped and closed his eyes against the image of blood and war. "But the worst thing? I'm shit-scared I'm about to mess up your life."

"Stop worrying about me. I'm not one of your fragile mermaids, you know. I'm tough, like you. And we haven't left everything." I nodded towards Anees, who had curled up on my brother's knees and fallen asleep.

"No." He stroked her hair dreamily. I wanted to remind him of all there was to look forward to but was unsure how to initiate such difficult topics of conversation. Years of secrets still lay between us.

"Farlo was leading a riot into Exer. I saw him. Bersha too," I said.

Instead of anger, my brother sniffed mournfully. "I didn't want to choose. I wanted him to come! I know why he wants war. I get it! But it's worth risking all. War has no happy end. Not for people like us."

"Not for anyone. You knew about Farlo?"

He traced the outline of Anees's ear with his finger. "I talked with him. Tried to anyway. Maybe one day, he'll listen. I hope he'll wait for my word before fighting. But—I can't do more."

I tutted and pulled the parcels Will had given me from my bag and spread them out on the empty seat. "I don't know if I can open them. It'll make me cry."

"I'm in the same place about Farlo," Korl said.

"Rubbish. Farlo is poison, but my friends aren't," I retorted, but my brother wouldn't be drawn into an argument.

"I hope you didn't bring the scissors."

I unwrapped Will and Eileen's box first. A thick wad of notes lay inside and a tiny sand-filled bottle. I was aghast at the cash and immediately closed the lid. "I can't take this! We need to get the next train back to Breen. Why have they given me money? It must be all their savings."

Korl didn't say anything, only passed a tissue while I blubbed. When the ticket collector appeared, I silently handed over cash and made a mental pact to one day repay their kindness and trust.

Thanks to Will and Eileen, our journey was easy and carefree. Instead of hiding from ticket guards, we bought endless snacks and drinks. The guards taught us new card games, and asked questions about Breen. They made us their favourites instead of chasing us.

The journey took days. I intermittently slept and then awoke to mess around again with my brother. Despite the strangeness of the situation and the uncertainty about our future, I was positive and happy.

Relentlessly, I tried to uncover the truth Anees and

Farlo had spoken of, but Korl told me little about Craw.

"Wait, Devi. Yes? Soon you'll find out. I have to speak to Jon first. It's not only our lives that depend on what I say. Okay? Soon, you'll know more than you wanted. I promise."

"Fine."

"Have you two stopped arguing? I never thought I'd see the day," Anees said.

"For now. Can you smell the sea yet?"

FINALLY, THE TRAIN pulled into a station with a board that spelled *Craw. Speak-and-Listen.* We wearily clambered off and followed the signs to a nearby office. I was cowed and shrank back from the crowds and officials who stood talking. My brother wasn't so timid. He strolled up to the booth and announced our arrival.

"The Krakens are here."

His voice boomed across the hall. Instantly, the chattering and noise died down, and every person turned. I grabbed at Anees's arm and held on.

A beaming official with a clipboard soon appeared. She patted my shoulder as if she knew me, and I found myself grinning back. Her welcome was warm and genuine and did much to ease my worries.

"Welcome, Krakens! My name's Adu. I'm your liaison, and I'm going to look after you. We're going to take you to your accommodation now. I'll be overseeing your stay. Don't worry about anything at all. I'm so very happy to see you."

We were taken by bus to a small cottage they said was a few miles north of Craw. Along the way, we saw the barriers which contained much of the city. When my brother asked why we couldn't stay in the city, we were told about various restrictions.

"It's not quite ready," Adu said. "The water pipes don't work, and there's no power. Even the world's best engineers can't fix things. It's been impossible to rebuild under such circumstances. Some say it's due only to lack of materials and planning, others claim it's the curse of the Sea Mother."

My brother shook his head sadly. "I've heard about the myth. I wonder... Some things are stronger than what we can see and understand."

"Since the war, every living creature has abandoned Craw. Not even the crabs come ashore anymore. The sea was poisoned after the bomb, but all the years since have cleaned the seabed. There's no real reason why the animals don't return. We shall see." Adu looked as if she'd like to say more.

"I hope Sea Mother isn't relying on us," I said. "Since I don't believe in myths."

Adu smiled politely. "You don't, little sister? We think it's likely due to sea creatures having established new habitats, but it's not been easy. We can't find specialist workers prepared to come back. Craw is the guilty secret nobody wants to talk about. We hope the speak-and-listen will be an end to whatever curse has gripped Craw these thirteen years. I remember the sea when it was bursting with life. Craw beach is my home."

She opened the door to the cottage and handed the key to Anees. "Please treat this house as your own. Be comfortable and peaceful. The bus leaves from the street corner every hour. It will take you to a nearby town if you want to visit a beach and shops. There's food in the fridge and hopefully everything you need. I've left clothes and shoes but had to guess at the sizes. You're safe here."

"Where will the other visitors stay?" I asked.

Adu waved her arms around the street. "These houses are all available. This was built as a sport village many years ago and is now used as the trial hub. We don't know exactly how many visitors will attend, but we hope to fill the village. I'm staying at the yellow house at the end of the row with my partner, Luce. You might see our little dog, Bluebell. She'll be looking out for you and will probably visit you at night in your garden. Luce will certainly come by. If you get lost, she'll help you find your way home. Knock if you need anything. I'll call by in a few days. Otherwise, please rest. I'll see you the morning of the trial, and I promise to be with you afterwards. I'm your friend. You can count on me, and Luce."

My brother had stayed quiet throughout the chatter. He offered a hand to Adu and bowed. "Thank you. Thank you so much. I was worried about everything, but it's all been taken care of."

I'd never seen him so polite or formal, and started to laugh. Anees elbowed me sharply, so I stifled my mirth.

"But what about my cousin?" I asked. "Can we visit him? It's been so long. I want to know he's all right."

Adu bit her lip and shuffled her feet from side to side. "I'm sorry. The defendants have requested to be apart until the speak-and-listen."

"But why?" I said, deflated and disappointed that after all the weeks apart, we still wouldn't be reunited.

Adu shrugged. "It's a difficult time. We've tried to make it as stress-free as we can, but still. Perhaps they wish to offer you space and time? Maybe he wants to make sure you speak as you truly wish and not because you feel pressure."

"Oh," I said.

Adu patted my shoulder. "I shouldn't tell you this, but—your cousin knows you're arriving today. I told him about the applications myself. He was especially pleased when I read your name. Very, very pleased. He's been waiting for the train to know you're safely arrived. I shall tell him you're here now. Sister, you're our youngest speaker, the same age I was when we left Craw." She leaned forward and kissed my cheek warmly.

I lost composure and cried. "Sorry. I wanted to see Jon," I said.

She wiped my tears away and hugged me. "I understand better than you might think. Craw stirs many memories! Have hope. I know this place so well. We came back more than a year ago, and it was a painful ruin compared to how it used to be. In the last few months, though, we've seen a change. The air smells different, and the birds sing new tunes. Even the sand is changing. All will be well. I'm sure of it. Hold on a little while longer, honey. *She will rise.*"

"All right. There is one thing we need—have you got any hand cream?" I asked.

"I'll get some," she promised.

We said goodbye and went into the cottage, where Anees tried out the beds and opened the many cupboards. "It's amazing," she said excitedly. "Look at this! I think it's a bikini!"

CHAPTER EIGHTEEN

THE BEACH AND waters near our house were rich and plentiful with creatures: dolphins, seals, jellyfish and crabs, fish, emperor shrimp, sea horses, and zebra turkeyfish. I thought about what Adu had said about the sea surrounding Craw being emptied of life and hoped it wasn't true.

We spent the days before the trial in a happy, hazy bubble far removed from the courts. Korl and I recognised many of the creatures by name and were soon reacquainted with the oceanic landscape. Anees was much absorbed gazing at birds with sing-song cries and swooping shrieks. Some would swoop down and land on her shoulder.

"I haven't forgotten after all, and neither have they," she said. "Birds are my family! They remember. Isn't it amazing?"

I awoke to the squabbles of gulls and couldn't wait to get back down to the beach to greet them. "I'm coming," I called, throwing on some clothes and only pausing to eat when Korl insisted.

The only evidence Craw existed was a high metallic barrier enclosing the city and even sliced through the beach and into the sea. It didn't fit with the landscape. When the sun shone, the barrier glowed. We tried to ignore it, but it permeated my thoughts. Sometimes, I walked beside it with my hand running along its unnatural surface.

"Don't do that," my brother said.

"Why?" I asked and banged the wall with my knuckles. A hollow echo returned my knock.

"I don't know," Korl said. "It unnerves me. Knock. Don't knock. I don't care, Devi Bee."

He got out his pencils and sat by the rockpools to draw. Anees and I bathed and chatted. Dressed in the orange bikini, she was as exotic as the fantastical creatures within the ocean.

"In case he doesn't say, you look lovely," I said.

She splashed me with freezing sea water. "So do you."

At night, we cooked and sat outside in the sheltered garden. As Adu had promised, a sweet dog visited and made herself at home. She took a special liking to Anees and even stayed overnight, curled up on her bed.

Sometimes, Adu also called by with a tall woman called Luce. They brought gifts and food and told stories of lands far away.

On the first night Luce visited, Anees took one look at her and then gasped and sobbed. The two hugged and laughed; it was clear they'd already met, years before. They walked slowly together down the beach and came back beaming.

One night, Adu asked if we'd visited Berker Park.

"Yes! I went just before we left."

She gripped Luce's hand. They leaned forward and asked together.

"Did you see our mermaids?"

"Of course. I looked at every one and even into the hollow rooms inside. What was their purpose?"

Luce told us the history of the statues at Berker. "Many Crawians escaped inside those statues. Adu and I helped to paint and get them ready. When it was time, people hid inside, and we sealed the doors. The mermaids were transported through the city gates without the guards knowing of the people hiding. It was terrifying. We never knew how many of our friends would survive. Not until years later, when people started to regroup."

She smiled and hid tears. "We were lucky. All our mermaids survived, and so did the people inside."

Luce rubbed the little dog behind the ears. "And this one too! Bluebell came with us from Craw, all those years ago. We wouldn't have gotten away if it weren't for her. Those mermaids are family to us. When the statues left the factory in Craw, it was a great victory. Driven by trucks and trains as big as houses. The guards didn't guess there were people inside. Until they did! We escaped in an air balloon just as the bomb exploded. Days later, we arrived in darkness at Berker Park. When the time is right, we'll raise the mermaid balloon and light up the skies once more. This time, I insist you come, Anees."

Luce and Anees exchanged a hug. I looked around to

see my brother's reaction to the story, but he was at the far end of the garden struggling to build a barbecue and didn't hear.

We talked into the early hours of the morning. I played with and stroked Bluebell, who liked to curl up on a lap. It was almost dawn by the time Luce and Adu left. Bluebell stayed behind with us.

Anees took pity on my brother and built the barbecue.

"I don't want to eat fish or meat anymore," she said, eyeing the fire. "In Exer, I was hungry, and there was no choice. We're equal creatures and should look out for one another. Every being is connected, and every life precious. I can't eat my kin!"

"Me either," Korl said.

I looked at the swooping bats and agreed. We cooked some vegetables and fruits instead.

"He'd do anything you say," I said.

"I would," Korl said, swiping me with a fly swatter.

It soon became apparent I'd never really known either of them. Under the bright moonshine, I discovered many illuminating facts. My brother was teaching Anees to read, and in turn, she taught him to mimic, and understand, birdsong.

Away from Exer City, all things seemed brighter. From how my brother relaxed, it was clear he was similarly affected by our new surroundings.

"Wouldn't it be nice if all the Exers could come back here? Start again and love ourselves?" I said.

We talked endlessly about Jon, retelling stories of his birthday cakes and games. It was easier to talk about those times than the more difficult subjects. My brother sometimes clammed up and would say no more.

"What made you decide to come here?" I asked him.

"A lot of things. I always wanted to do the right thing. But not if it meant Exers would die. For a long time, I didn't know what the right thing was."

"And?" I said, seeing there was more.

He smiled and stroked Bluebell behind the ear, as she liked. "One day, I saw these little kids playing in the street. They each had one of our mermaids."

"*Your* mermaids. I was only part of them by force," I said, reminded of the nights spent carrying heavy sacks.

"And they started singing the Sea Mother rhyme. You know the one?"

"Yeah, yeah, yeah. Get on with it." I nodded, impatient to hear the rest.

"They looked up into the sky and held hands. So sweet, and pure. I knew what to do." He finished the story and kissed Bluebell's head.

Expecting something more, the explanation irritated me intensely. "Shitting hell. What? That's it?"

My brother shrugged but wouldn't rise to the bait or argue. "Can't wait to see Jon." He prodded me with his big toe. "Stop swearing."

Although he was close, it seemed to me our cousin remained far away. The uncertainty of the trials still lay between us, and the court was as unknown as the barrier shielding Craw.

"What do you think Jon's doing?"

"If he's got any sense, he'll be at a beach with a hunky man. Jon's quite a catch," Korl said.

"Probably. Everyone's kissing except me!"

I missed Ren terribly and began to wonder if my friend had been a dream. Often, I examined her parcel but wasn't able to open it because I wanted the last connection saved for a while longer.

"I'm sure she'll be here soon if she said so," Anees said. "So many visitors are arriving! Every day, there are more."

The houses around ours began to overspill with people from all creeds and from all corners of Mainland. At first, we shied away, sure they would be suspicious, perhaps even dangerous. Instead, they nodded respectfully and offered gifts of fruits and flowers from the lands left behind.

My brother proved particularly talkative and interested in countries beyond our knowledge. He surprised me often by initiating conversations and popping into other houses.

"Looks like everyone was waiting for this chance," he said thoughtfully.

On the last day before the speak-and-listen, we set off for the beach with a picnic. When we climbed off the bus, I ran down the dune path and onto the beach like always. I could never wait to throw off my shoes and feel the warmth of the sand between my toes.

The glittering sea stretched beyond. "Look at this!" I shouted back at my brother, who made his way more cautiously over the dunes.

Too impatient to wait, I skidded down the beach, wearing new shorts provided by Adu, who saw to our every need. I tore off my clothes and paddled in without looking at anything but the blue expanse of water.

When someone approached, I didn't pay much attention. We'd become used to the many visitors and had grown accustomed to chatting with people from all creeds.

When a hand gripped mine, I turned to face Ren, looking like she'd walked straight from the ocean.

She laughed and grabbed my hands joyfully. "Devora! I thought it was you!"

For ages, we sat at the edge of the waves with water trickling over our toes. "Will told me you'd gone," I said.

"I knew you'd be here. Don't ask me how. I knew it the day we met," Ren said. "I dreamt you and I were merfolk, swimming under the water. You look gorgeous, by the way."

"So do you."

The awkwardness vanished into the sparkling waters, and eventually, she led me back up the beach to where her parents sat with Korl and Anees. It seemed only I was nervous as the four talked enthusiastically and without apparent awkwardness.

I held out my hand. "Good morning. It's lovely to meet you."

Ren's Ma stood and laughed at my hand. When she pulled me into a gigantic hug, I knew it would be all right.

"Sit down and have some lunch," she said. "I want to know all about you. Now we've found you, maybe Ren will stop moaning. We've scoured every single inch of this beach looking for a gorgeous Devora."

I tried to appear oblivious to the compliment, even as my cheeks burned up.

"It's true," Ren's da said. "Call us Shena and Hune. No need to be nervous. Your brother and Anees have told us all about everything. It sounds amazing. Everything's amazing."

I saw where Ren had got her easy manners and ways of talking. I joined the conversation and asked questions about their work and lives.

"I missed you," Ren said, not even trying to whisper.

"Me too," I admitted.

"What are your hopes for tomorrow?" Shena asked, opening a bottle of cider and offering it round.

"I don't honestly know," I said. "I thought coming here would be hard and horrible. It's been the opposite. I keep thinking I should feel bad, and then I feel guilty. I'm rested and can't wait to see my cousin."

Shena nodded vigorously. "Good. I must say, the councils have prepared well for the days ahead. I heard they consulted with people from all creeds. The speak-and-listen is about the past, yes, and also the future. Nobody wants Craw to remain a barren wasteland. And Mainland without unity or treaties between countries! The last thirteen years have seen cruelty and inequality, racism and hatred. It's time for change and where better than Craw? We'll hear some difficult things, no doubt, but the good news is there'll be roomfuls of people wanting to help."

She drank deeply from the bottle and then burped. "And how are you both feeling?"

My brother shook his head thoughtfully. "Feel? Talk? Participate? They're all new things for us. I only hope the day doesn't overwhelm us. Our cousin struggles with words. I guess we all do. Sometimes, I panic. I can't believe we're here, and it's not a trap. I want to—but I just can't." He gazed out at sea.

"Not yet. But soon," Anees murmured.

Not for the first time since our arrival, I was struck by my brother's capacity for explaining what I'd struggled to put into words.

"You're doing all right," I told him.

"I admired the Exer tunnels very much," Shena said. "A vibrant way to keep the past alive. Each time, I was affected."

My brother had a swig of the cider, then coughed and spluttered. "I'll be glad when the speak-and-listen is over, and we can make plans. Is it too much to hope for? Maybe I shouldn't try to think ahead."

"Over?" Shena said. "It won't be over. There's a city to fix, waiting to be opened up. *Your* city. You're as responsible as anyone for what comes next. It's the way of the Crawian. With the ocean, we stand as one. The minute we stopped, look at what happened. Mainland is looking to these trials. If we're successful, then the whole world can benefit."

I waited for Korl to point out we were still banned from Craw and had a permit to stay for the duration of the speak-and-listen only.

He nodded, pulled Anees into his arms, and discussed ideas about how Craw might be rebuilt. It was clear he'd already thought far beyond the next few weeks. The change of attitude was heartening and inspirational. I too wanted to believe we might have a future alongside the sea.

The beach soon filled with families and people of all creeds. We buried Korl up to his neck in the sand and positioned a flower behind his ear. Shena showed us how to make boats from reeds and structures from nothing but sand and water. I'd never had so much fun and only wished Jon were with us. When the time came to get back on the bus, I didn't want to part with Ren again and refused to let her go.

"A few more minutes? I haven't opened the parcel yet," I said.

"Open it in the morning and take it with you tomorrow," she replied. "It will help you say what you want."

"I wish I even knew what that was. I wish I could fast-forward time to when it's all over, and we could be two girls having fun."

"Only be for a little while," Shena said. "Tomorrow, we'll be there in the great hall with you. I think you'll soon be seeing each other every day."

That night, I slept deeply and dreamt of merfolk and a gate under the waters locked with an iron padlock.

CHAPTER NINETEEN

UNTIL MIDNIGHT WHEN I awoke to a scrabbling at the window and stones rebounding off the glass.

"Devora!" a voice called from the direction of the garden. "Are you there?"

I stumbled to the window and peered out. My room was on the first floor, but it wasn't far up from garden level, so I could make out the shape of someone hiding behind the lavender bush.

"Who is it?" I whispered loudly.

A shape with a vast bubble of frizzy hair stepped out from the undergrowth and beckoned me down. Through the darkness, I saw it was Ren.

I dressed and hurried through the cottage as quietly as I could. In Exer City, I wasn't allowed out at night unless

Korl or Anees accompanied me. Unlocking the door and slipping out into the night to meet Ren felt wildly exciting.

"If Korl sees me," I began.

"Let's run," she whispered and pulled me away from the cottage in the direction of the beach.

Only when we reached the barrier preventing anyone from entering the Craw beach did we stop and catch our breath.

"Is it really you? I couldn't sleep, and it seemed wrong you were so near our cottage," she said. "I can't wait until we can be together whenever we want."

"It's me," I said.

"Good. I've got something to show you."

She led me along a narrow path adjacent to the barrier. It was overgrown with weeds and stingy nettles and didn't look like the kind of place anyone should venture.

"To Craw central. Of course," she said.

"Are we allowed?" I tried to jump over the longest stingers. "I've heard there's a horrible and deadly disease, and anyone who tries to enter will either die of the rot or be stopped by law enforcement. Let's go the other way?"

"No, we're not allowed. That's why we're going. I found this the other day with Ma and decided you needed to see it."

"What is it?"

We reached a track where the path bordered the cliffs, and we had to stand back, close to the barrier, to avoid slipping downwards into the rocks. I became breathless with fear.

"We should go back," I said.

The wind howled, and a strange screaming came from

far below, where the sea crashed against rocks.

"Is this safe?" I shouted through the roar.

"No," she shouted back gleefully. "We could plummet into the sea. Aren't you sick of being safe?"

I followed her along the narrow pathway with my hands flat against the barrier and my breath coming in ragged gasps. There was no time to worry about law enforcers or where the path led, and I concentrated on not slipping on the crumbling pathway.

Finally, the track grew wider to a torn section of barrier eroded by the weather. Ren climbed in through the opening, and I followed. The instant we stepped away from the cliff and onto firmer ground, the wind stopped, and the supernatural screaming faded into the more familiar noises of crickets and grasshoppers.

"What was that?" I said, relieved to be on stable land. "It sounded like screaming. Where are we?"

I looked around, expecting to sense disease and destruction. Beyond the barrier lay endless dark streets and silent houses with shuttered windows, like hundreds of staring eyes. A scent of oranges and rose permeated the air.

"Cool, right?" Ren said. "Not what you expected?"

"We shouldn't be here. It's supposed to be sick and diseased," I said uneasily, looking for evidence of my statement. "Maybe the air's full of rot because the water won't flow in from the sea."

"It's what I wanted you to see," she said excitedly. "Come."

She took my hand and led me farther into the city. The sounds of our footsteps echoed into the night, and I found myself trying to step more quietly so as not to wake anything sleeping.

"Shh," I said. "We're making too much noise."

"Why? Nobody cares. I think Craw's happy to see us. It's been too long." In the middle of a wide street, she spun me round, faster and faster until we were giddy with laughter. "Hear us? It's Ren and Devora!" she shouted into the still city.

Her voice caught on the wind and echoed through the empty streets before being soaked up. The buildings seemed to want us there, as she'd said.

"We're here!" I shouted, too, and forgot to listen for law enforcers. Perhaps the midnight heat and tiredness made me so reckless. We raced around the streets as if we owned them and discovered abandoned parks with swings moving in the wind. Once again, the sight of the movement was neither frightening nor spooky. Instead, I pushed Ren high in the air on a swing and then shot down the slide head first.

"It's so bizarre. An empty playground should be a sad thing."

"But it isn't," Ren finished for me. "That's what I wanted to show you. Coming here the other night made me so happy. I don't understand it. I think Craw's been waiting for us to come back."

"Yeah. I hope so."

Although nobody had legal entry, the houses looked tended, covered with baskets of flowers and grapevines overflowing with plump fruit.

"It doesn't look abandoned," I said.

"Because it isn't. A man told us people sneak in all the time and have planted flowers and fruits. Up to this year, nothing would grow."

I picked a grape and bit into the juicy fruit. "It's growing now. Adu told me she and Luce are allowed in. Maybe they planted the flowers?"

After a time, we entered a zone filled with stumps of stone. I tripped and landed on my bottom. "What are they?"

"Ma said she thinks they're where the statues used to stand."

"The ones at Berker?"

"All over. The artist sent them all over the world, so her legacy wouldn't be forgotten. There's a rumour she's coming to the trials."

"Maybe she knows Luce and Adu? They escaped Craw inside one of the mermaid vessels."

After a while, we arrived at a large square filled with scientific equipment. I bent to read a dial. "What's this?"

"I think it's where engineers are testing the conditions or something. Ma heard they test the air quality and the water every week."

In the middle of the square, we found a large ring of tiles bearing the pattern of waves and fish. It was peppered with holes.

"It's the fountain!" Ren said. "I've read about it. The children used to run in and out of the jets."

We traced the outlines of the jets and came to a metallic box filled with dials and graphs.

Ren pointed to a central shape. "What's the red button for? See how it has a tiny mermaid painted in the middle?"

"I'm not sure," I said.

We stared for a while. I didn't meet her eye, but I knew she was thinking the same thing as me. When she caught my hand, I nodded. Together, we pressed the red button and then waited for a while.

The noise began so gradually we dismissed it as breeze or the nearby ocean.

For the first time, we became frightened and huddled together.

"It's the law enforcers," I gasped. "We should hide."

But it was too late. The marching became louder until it was a deafening howl. I covered my ears with my hands and wished we'd never come.

It had started at the far side of the circle. At first, a tap, and then another, and soon the hundreds of drips replaced the roar. When the first jet exploded, we both screamed. I reached for Ren, and she for me.

Powerful streams blasted into the night like fireworks and arched across the sky before cascading back down. The strength of the water caused the ground to shake, and a few pots fell over and broke, and small animals scurried away.

"Sea Mother's giving birth," Ren said.

With each new jet, hope flooded my body. "If water could return to Craw, maybe Exers could too? What does it mean? Why has this happened now after so many years?"

"It means Craw wants you back. All these years, it was waiting for the children to come home. Sea Mother heard you, Devora. Didn't you hear her shouting?"

"I heard something, yes. I don't believe in mermaids."

"You've only forgotten to listen to what you know is true," Ren said.

We stayed for hours watching the water and bearing witness to the transformation of Craw until, finally, darkness began to lift.

"Come," Ren said. "One last thing before the speak-and-listen."

"I don't want to leave in case the water never returns ever again. I'm so tired. I feel like we've walked here all the way from Breen."

We stumbled back towards the sea and followed the early-morning calls of gulls and old signs still attached to walls. I noticed what it had been too dark to see when we arrived—the many signs showing Craw was blooming with growth: Families of stoats and geese, foxes and badgers scurried for home. Everywhere, the green shoots of new flowers and plants blossomed.

Down at the beach, the barrier glinted in the weak sun as a reminder of the many changes necessary before Craw could be repaired.

"Even if the water is flowing again, the sea is still poisoned," I said.

"We'll see. Soon, you'll believe."

We took off our shoes and ran to the calm grey-blue where waves rolled and crashed rhythmically, and everywhere was the scent of bitter salt. The hypnotic rise and roll of waves began to affect my vision.

I rubbed my eyes, and when I looked again, something looked right back at us.

"What is it?" Ren said.

"The water doesn't look diseased." I strained my eyes to look into the distance. "Is that...?"

Far away on the horizon, black shapes grew closer.

"Do you see?" Ren shouted, jumping up and down.

"They've come home. Seals and dolphins!"

I stripped first and stepped into the freezing waters as naked as the merfolk. Ren soon followed suit. We tripped over pebbles and shouted against pain until we were fully submerged. But for the coldness of the water, I would have thought it a dream.

"Sea Mother? Do you hear us?" I shouted into the spray and the tumble of water and sea life.

Shield Diary Ten
Korl

We snake through ancient doors that kept us safe from invaders, fires, and rampaging armies, but not from the betrayal of adults. I take the keys from Jon and lock the doors behind us.

"Why?" he says.

"Because we can use it to bargain. We give the army the keys if they promise to sort the mess out. No more killing. We can't sort it out, but they can. It's the International Army!"

"Yeah. That's good, Korl. Let's do it."

Jon's talking again. We walk along the walled corridor, with fresh air on our faces. The little kids don't speak. They're looking above at the birds and the sunshine, the butterflies with blue wings. Devi chases one.

When we reach the bridge, I think of my ma. "We have to take off our shirts. You at the front and me at the back."

When he strips, I see how thin my cousin is. He waits

for a few seconds, holding Devi's hand tightly. The snake draws breath. From the back, I can see Jon's shirt. It's dirty and there's blood, but it's mostly white.

"I'll go first," Jon says. "Stay here until I reach the other side. If I don't wave, go back."

"Don't go, Jon." I'm crying again, painful wracking sobs.

Arlo hugs me. "It'll be okay. They won't shoot him. It's international law."

"Don't you leave me?"

"Never," Arlo says.

Jon walks tall, shirt up in the air. Across the bridge, without slowing or stopping. Not once does he cry or shake.

They don't shoot him.

They don't shoot him.

He turns and waves.

I grip Devi. "Let's go. Don't you let go of my hand."

We walk, single file, across the bridge I used to cross on Sundays with my parents. At the other side of the bridge, an army of green and no smiles wait for us.

"Into the vans," the army man says. "Quick now."

"What are you going to do? Don't shoot anyone. Please?" I beg.

"We do not beg!" Arlo says.

I hand the army man the keys to the Gatehouse and Craw, our families and history.

"If I give you these, promise you won't shoot anyone? Please, bring it to an end. Promise me."

He takes the keys. "I'll bring it to an end."

"Korl!" Farlo screams. "Don't leave me!"

I don't see what happens to the other kids. To Arlo,

Oosha and Nila, Fralo, Heva, and all the other shields I love with all my heart. They get loaded onto trucks and vans, and I can't do anything but watch. At least they've got one another. Arlo makes them hold hands and waves from the back.

Jon grips my hand. "Korl, come. You got them out. You can't do everything. They'll be okay. Arlo will look after them now."

A soldier lifts me, Jon, and Devi into a van. Devi starts singing, and then we do too.

I feel, again.

Bad, about Arlo.

Glad, we're alive.

Upset, about Ma and Da.

I feel.

"They'll feed us once we get there," Jon says. "We're kids. They'll take care of us."

"Where's there?" I ask.

"I don't know. Maybe a hospital or something?"

They drive us a few miles across the border into another country. To a building with white rooms and people with kind faces. They lock the door. They don't speak our language, but they smile and teach us some words. They bring us food and drink, books and games. It's warm. It's not too bad. I've got Jon and Devi.

We sleep.

I feel.

It happens. The shining light of victory booms and shakes the bars on the windows, the floors, and windows. The prison lights up. Jon and Devi are fast asleep. I climb up onto the window ledge and look through the bars.

For a lonely minute, a shape goes past. It's a huge balloon in the sky! I know it's Arker Fi, reminding me not to forget. I never will.

"I see you! I see you!" I start humming the old sea ballad. Who knew it was true?

One last time, I hear Arker.

"I'll be waiting for you, Korl," she says. "Don't forget. I'll come back for you."

And then I don't hear her anymore

I wish I was on the balloon with Arker! I want to leave too.

When the floating mermaid in the sky goes by and keeps on going, far away, Craw goes dark. Rain that looks like poison hammers the windows.

I feel too much, too much.

It goes dark.

You don't realise how dark the world can go. How it gets into your head, and you can't get it out again.

You stop feeling.

"What was it?" you ask a guard.

He answers in broken Crawian. "A bomb to end the war. It's over. Don't worry. Go to sleep. You're safe."

You snuggle up with Jon and Devi and drift off to sleep. At the back of your mind, you know it's not over, not forever. One day, one day, one day.

When all-a world goes dark, look up,
To find me in the skies.
Close not thine heart,
Or dim thy voice,
Sea Mother, she shall rise.

CHAPTER TWENTY

I LEFT THE beach reluctantly with scratched legs and feet numbed from icy waters. I was exhausted and raw, Ren, serene and warm.

"How did you know the city was alive?" I asked her. "You never doubted, did you?"

"I've always known I was a part of the air and water as much as of people. It's hard to explain. I hear things more loudly than others do. You give off a lot of noise, and I picked it up. I'm a sea sponge," she said seriously.

"I agree!"

We watched the sun appear from behind the horizon and the dark sky turn pink and ripe with promise of a glorious day. Underneath such bold colour, I felt tiny yet connected to the world.

"We've always been part of things, Devora, as everyone is. Now you truly know it. The door was there, but you weren't ready to open it."

"Ren with the double you—you'll be there today? Do you promise?"

"I'll be there, girl! Remember what we've seen tonight and have faith. Life and the sea are here. Not *coming* back or waiting for us to give the go-ahead. The day will be okay. I know it. Trust me. Even when times have been bad, I knew *this* day was waiting. Sea Mother won't let us down, nor will your family."

Her ardent words gripped me, and it wasn't easy to walk away from the scenes we'd witnessed.

I crept into the cottage and silently dressed. A while later, my dishevelled brother appeared from his bedroom.

"What are you doing up so early, with hair a fright and a red face, Devi Bee? You look like a tomato that's escaped from a haystack." He collapsed from his joke, laughing harder when I offered my most stern of expressions.

"Er—nothing. No, nothing. Do you think it will be all right, today? I don't want to go. I wish it was over."

My brother reached across and dampened down my spiky hair. "I'll be there. Jon and Anees too. I won't let anything happen to you."

I opened my mouth, looked again at my brother's hairy legs, and clamped it back shut.

"You look wiped out. 'Er, nothing all night,' eh?" Korl said. "Sounds suspicious."

"I've got to get ready."

I grunted and switched on the coffee machine before sorting through my six-page document. It was lovingly arranged in chronological- and colour-code order. "Gods. Will I ever be ready?" I muttered.

Korl watched with raised eyebrows. "Do you think you've got enough?"

"Shut up! I've spent weeks getting it ready. Don't you think there's enough?"

I dropped the whole lot, and the papers scattered across the tiled floor.

My brother knelt to help and then drew back when I slapped his hands away. "I was joking. Calm down, Devi. It'll be all right. Why are you suddenly spooked? I was spooked weeks ago, but now I'm okay. Why now?"

"This is Jon's *life we*'re talking about. Our teacher says they can enforce a sentence. What if he gets a sentence and we never see him again?"

"Not going to happen. Can't you tell by the way they've treated us? They want the speak-and-listen to be the start of a new Craw, not the end." He reached forward and tugged my nose.

"Well, you've changed your tune," I retorted huffily. It was irritating he'd transcended the Exer psychology of expecting the worst, yet I hadn't, especially since he'd initiated much of the paranoia.

"Doesn't mean I'm not worried about today though." He ruffled his hair with hands almost cleared of cuts and bruises.

I caught his wrist and examined his fingers. "Your hands are healed?"

"Yes, all better. Anees's too. Thanks to you."

"*Are* you worried?"

"Not worried, but watchful. I don't want to let Jon

down, obviously. I certainly don't want to be responsible for the future of hundreds of people. It's hard enough being your older brother! My days as leader are over, Devi. I never enjoyed being in charge, whatever you might think."

"I wish Jon weren't first to stand." On an impulse, I kissed his wrist. "You're a fine older brother. Mostly."

Anees wandered in with her hair wrapped in a towel. "Everything happens for a reason. Listen to the birds. Don't you hear? Jon is up first because the Krakens will lead the way. It's destined to be so. It always was. I think I knew it the first time we met."

I made a non-committal grunt. "Today isn't going to be easy. It wouldn't be so bad if it weren't being broadcast over Mainland."

"Are you worried about that? I'll sort it," Korl said.

I was more worried Jon would be watching when I stood to offer my defence than of unknown viewers from other lands. "And why did they have to go and invite so many?"

"Because it's time to stop being ashamed," Anees said. "Every person in the audience had a part in what happened. Their story is also our story. Every being is connected, Devi. Anyway, I better get dressed." She wandered back into the bedroom she shared with Korl.

I wondered if I, too, had changed. "She seems? I don't know. So different."

"Remember, whatever you hear today, Jon and I loved you and wanted you safe. It was a long time ago. It's in the past. Gone. What you'll hear isn't new, though it might sound that way."

The *L* word was uncomfortable to hear. I looked away,

but my brother took my chin and held me still.

"Hear me? Our parents loved you. Jon and I loved you. We still love you. It's forever."

"Yeah, yeah, I know. Are *you* ready? What are you going to say?"

He perched on the edge of the table and fiddled with his shirt buttons.

"Korl?" I snapped waspishly.

"Well, it depends on what Jon wants. I need to ask his permission and won't drag things up that are best left. I wish I could have planned what to say *with* him."

"But if he'd stayed in Exer, you wouldn't have come," I pointed out.

"True."

Anees returned, and our conversation dried up. Instead of her usual black clothing, she wore a dress bearing a pattern of birds. The outfit was so perfect for the day I could have cried. In comparison, my outfit comprised a dark trouser suit with waistcoat and matching hat I thought made me look serious and mature. I realised I looked ridiculous and decided to change into jeans and a T-shirt.

"Look at you," my brother said adoringly.

"What? Is it all right?" Anees asked.

"I don't know what I did to be so lucky."

"Yuk," I said, secretly touched at his words and gentle manner. "Yes, I'm ready. I'm going to be a proper law enforcer and offer facts and evidence. In case it's needed. Jon will be proud of me." I almost lost my composure. To cover it up, I seized the hat and determinedly placed it on my head.

"Whatever are you wearing? Won't you be hot?" Korl said, gazing at the black hat with shaking shoulders.

I decided I would stay dressed in the suit after all. "Oh, shut up. What would you know about what law enforcers wear? At least one of us looks professional." I grabbed my files. "It's not too late for me to cut a dolphin into your shirt."

"Don't be a muffin," he said.

We bickered all the way down the lane and only stopped when the bus appeared. It was then I severely lost my cool. By the time we arrived, emotion and exhaustion had taken hold, and I locked myself in the bathroom with Ren's parcel.

Lovingly wrapped in shiny tissue was a shrivelled sea flower with a card attached saying it came from the seabed near Craw and would bud when the time was right. I held it up to my ear and imagined the voice of the Sea Mother and the waves of Craw. For a few seconds, I allowed myself to drift mentally back to the previous night when I'd been so sure everything would turn out well.

Her other gift was a poem with loopy writing on scented yellow paper. In the corners of the page, she'd added images of smiling fish. I pictured her writing, surrounded by the coloured stones she loved. I felt better and slipped it into my jacket pocket.

Korl and Anees stood in front of the harsh barrier, which blocked off the beauty of Craw and now seemed incongruous and wrong. Compared to the wildness of the ocean, the cold metal was as harsh and illogical as the reasons that had led to the wars.

"What's the actual purpose of the barriers?" I asked the man who'd led us from the bus. "By whose orders is it there?"

He shook his head and grimaced. "Craw isn't safe."

I knew the explanation was untrue. Ren and I'd seen

nothing in the city which could cause harm. "Can't we just look?"

He scratched his head. "I'm afraid not. The answer—the one I'm meant to give—is because it's too dangerous. The buildings are unsafe. Disease is in the air." He shifted his feet uneasily.

There'd been nothing wrong with the buildings; many of the streets had looked recently renovated and cleared.

"What's the real answer?" Korl said.

The man looked behind at the long lines of people arriving in buses and cars. "The city bears our shame. Craw is nothing but an empty graveyard now. The broken toys of greedy people who didn't listen. We don't deserve to go back inside until we've atoned and Sea Mother invites us. We are but visitors, after all."

He insisted we didn't want to be late and should hurry along. My questions died away, and I felt subdued and chilled. The weight of the speak-and-listen thundered down, and I was glad to move off.

Under the bright sunshine, we followed the metal until arriving at a massive set of gates. The guard there stood back and indicated we should go inside. "Into the hall. Halt the tide!"

"Thank you. See you soon." I smiled as we passed and wanted to say something to give him hope. "It won't be long. My brother will make things right. Don't give up hope."

The gates caught my attention, and I examined the heavy wood carved with merfolk. For a while, we traced the figurines and admired the depictions of sea life.

"Feel the heartbeat? Don't the figures seem familiar? I'm sure we've seen them before, though I don't remember,"

Korl said, echoing my thoughts.

Finally, we entered a large circular area filled with stone merfolk. I became itchy with nerves.

"They've gone to so much trouble for us," I said.

"You okay, Devi?" Anees offered me a hand. "Remember this is for their benefit as much as ours. We don't have to feel beholden. The speak-and-listen isn't a festival or a condemnation. Think of today as the start of a conversation."

She stood tall and proud and shook back her red hair. When she nodded towards the officials, they bowed to her.

"Yeah. I will," I said, wishing I, too, had confidence and grace.

The noise hushed, and everyone looked our way. We walked in a line past the mermaids into a large reception area filled with flowers and baskets of fruits. There were many families and people of all types. I noticed the children being handed lollipops and felt comforted. Their parents wouldn't have let them come if the day was destined to be horrific.

"Oh gods," I muttered.

Korl led us to a lady holding a clipboard bearing the name "Kraken." She beamed as we approached and offered us water and gifts of small lavender bags in the shape of mermaids.

"Welcome! Are you Jon's family? He asked me to look out for you."

She hugged us each and kissed my cheeks. "Don't worry, darling! It's going to get much better now. You must be Devi. Jon wanted you to have this."

She attached a sweet little pin to my suit in the shape

and colours of a striped bumble bee.

The reminder of my childhood name cheered me immensely. "Thank you!" When I looked up, it was Korl and not I who had tears in his eyes.

"Devi Bumble Bee," he said. "Always buzzing and running. Never still."

"Take your time in there," the official said. "I'll see you during the breaks, I'm sure."

I'd been expecting a formal courtroom and was surprised when she led us through ornate blue doors into an outside circular area surrounded by stone seats with one area curtained off. I guessed it was where Jon and the other participants sat, and I ached to see him.

Despite the shadows of what was ahead, the serene open sky had a calming effect. Sun shone and birds flitted in and out of the many flowery baskets and trellises. From away to the east came the low but distinct crashing of waves on the beach, and there was a distinct smell of orange. It didn't feel like a place of horror but rather a garden of peace.

"I remember that smell," Korl said. "It's the orange buds."

"Me too," Anees said.

I met their eyes and grinned. For a few seconds, we joined together in a small circle.

"We're here. All the way from Exer! I wish they could see us now," I said.

"The worst is over," Korl said. "Maybe. I hope so."

He pulled Anees and me close and kissed us both. I was forced to admit my brother could be chivalrous and kind sometimes, though I would never tell him so.

The official pointed out a seating area covered with a

red cloth. "If you would like to sit here. When it's your turn to speak, you'll be called to the dais. Everything will be explained to you. Please let me know if there is anything you require and understand we are very pleased you're here. You're safe. Trust that whatever you say will be listened to without comment or judgement. This is a place of respect and voice."

She smiled, bowed, and winked at me. My brother and Anees bowed in return. I did the same, though it caused my hat to tumble onto the floor.

We sat upon the raised seats covered with felt. A device ran alongside every bench, which I guessed was an illuminator to display images and pictures. Luce, Adu, and Bluebell sat across the hall. I returned their waves, glad of their familiar and friendly faces.

The hall filled with onlookers and was soon alive with chatter. I heard the name Kraken whispered. It was clear everyone already knew who we were.

"Gods. Do you hear?" Korl whispered.

I thought about the TV back at Exer City and hoped I looked okay. "Why did I wear this silly suit?" I hissed.

Anees pointed to the centre. "That's where we speak? I don't need it. I'll stand and speak up into the sky. The birds will hear me. The sky will know."

The dais had a stone wall around and glass at the top shaped like a funnel. I'd seen a picture of something similar in history books about famous trials and war courts.

"I guess it's to project your voice," Korl muttered. "It looks fit for singers. What are we doing here? We don't belong."

I let go of the last shreds of my dignity and leaned into

his side. My brother responded by sliding an arm around my shoulders.

The crowds flocked in until the hall was full to bursting. Long cameras and lighting appeared around the dais. I thought of Will and Eileen, watching from so far away.

By the time everyone went quiet, I'd stilled my hands and willed myself to be brave. More than anything, I was afraid we'd all be useless to Jon.

Chapter Twenty-One

THE PROCEEDINGS BEGAN, and four people dressed in long blue gowns rose and asked for silence. The loud whispers and shuffling faded. A woman sang. Her voice rose and fell and was akin to waves and storms, but I felt detached and far away.

The singing heralded the start of the proceedings, and the curtain drew back to reveal my cousin Jon, who sat alone. The burst of emotion I'd anticipated didn't come.

He looked for us. I grinned and then stood on the bench and waved with both arms. My hat fell off again. A low murmur of laughter went around the hall.

"It's Jon!" I said loudly. "He's really here."

My cousin climbed up onto his bench and waved back. I forgot onlookers and the ruined city and experienced overwhelming relief my cousin was safe and alive.

He made our signs for how much he'd missed me, and I returned the gestures. No matter that hundreds of people stood between us; we communicated via our own language, created so long ago with Korl's book.

Finally, I sat back down, and the speaker introduced herself as the facilitator.

"I was once mayor. Now, I don't claim a title and have no right to do so. Thank you for coming, and welcome to the speak-and-listen. Over the next weeks, we welcome every story, song, and record of that war-torn time. We welcome those who claim to have done, and those who claim to have been done to. We welcome bus drivers and cleaners, rulers and royalty. Medics, street sweepers, builders, mothers, children, teachers, dancers, and craftspeople. Welcome, all! We shall listen without judgement. We hear. Each defendant is responsible for their own trial and sentence, if any. We demand quiet and respect. Our role is to facilitate and ensure your safety. After—we shall see. What comes next is up to us all. We do not advise, and we are not advisors."

She waited until every person in the room had nodded in acquiescence before going on.

It was about then I started to feel uncomfortable and perturbed by expensive flowers and flowing gowns, smiling faces and eagerness. The perfection of the surroundings made my head spin and my hands clench into fists. Sweat started pricking again at my neck.

I became fixated on the idea of destroying the flowers and tapestries and rampaging through the wooden benches until spent. Even to me, it didn't make sense, and I leaned into Anees for comfort.

The facilitator introduced us politely and with respect. I couldn't fault her, yet it was impossible to relax or feel easy.

"The day starts with the history of Jon Kraken who is one of the founders of the speak-and-listen. We thank Jon for all the time and energy he gave to helping us to set up this new method of dealing with war matters. As tradition dictates, it is our way to invite the Kraken family to begin."

We knew to expect this and had rehearsed what to do. Still, it was a shock. I slipped into a frantic daydream and returned when my brother pulled at the sleeve of my shirt.

"Devi. You're up. Are you all right? You don't have to go if you don't want."

"Yes." I clutched my file and made my way into the circle and the dais. I hadn't anticipated the wall would stand taller than me. "My name is Devora Kraken."

"We can't hear you or see anything but your hat," the facilitator said. "Can we fetch a chair for Devora to stand on?"

The crowd began to laugh and talk. Embarrassed, I shrank down and would willingly have died on the spot. By the time a chair was brought, I'd entirely lost my nerve and ran back to Korl.

"No. I'm not doing it. No, no."

I threw my hat on the floor and hid my face in my hands. My brother was furious. He climbed onto the bench and shouted so loudly the birds flocked away and the echoes of his anger lingered long in the atmosphere.

"This is my sister, Devora Kraken! She isn't here for your amusement or entertainment! Shut your mouths."

The laughter halted, and the hall went silent. The mood shifted from jolly to sombre, smug to pained. And with it, I started to feel better.

My brother snarled and glared as well as the most malevolent of sea creatures. Gone was the grovelling Exer, thankful for small mercies, and here was proud Crawian.

The facilitator bowed and wrung her hands. "I am so sorry and apologise deeply to Devora." She bowed to me and Korl. "Please, will you accept our apologies? I see we have got it wrong."

Away to the side, my cousin covered his face with a hand.

"Yes," I said. When they invited me to return to the dais, I declined.

My brother put his arms around me, and if I could have disappeared into the ground, I would have done.

"Don't worry." He kissed my head, reached for his bag, and made his way to the dais alone. "My name is Korl Kraken. I'll speak, but there are two conditions."

His voice projected across the hall as clear and forceful as stormy waves on the beach. With wild eyes and clenched fists and quite human, my brother glared as he spoke.

"Switch off the cameras and lock the doors! This is no show to be watched over popcorn! What I'm going to say is for my family, Exers, and the children of Craw. I know it will eventually end up in school papers and history leaflets, and that's okay. But for now—it stays here."

He crossed his arms and waited until the scurrying officials made a decision.

"We do as you ask," the facilitator said. "There will be no recordings. What happens here does not go further without your say-so."

My brother nodded. "So be it. I'm Jon's cousin. We've

been together, always. Forever! We learnt to fish and kick a ball together. I was with him as a shield child and have been with him since. Jon knows me better than anyone. He's closer to me in ways there are no words for."

He fixed his gaze intently at my cousin and brought his hand up to his chest.

"My second condition is down to him. I'm going to start by giving this book back. Jon, while you were away, I tidied it up and added some new pictures. I hope it's all right. It's yours."

Calmly, and with much dignity, Korl walked from the dais over to my cousin. When he reached Jon, they dissolved into a teary hug. I cried too. Although many wooden benches separated us, it was as if I were physically between the two men. I wished fervently we were back in our flat and had never come to this place of pomp and falseness. It seemed certain the revelations would damage us and reinforce the difficulties of our lives.

"It's all right," Anees whispered. "Trust him."

My brother briefly spoke to Jon and then walked back to the dais. I couldn't see what was agreed, but Jon nodded and made the sign for yes. Korl opened his bag and took out a small notebook.

"Jon has agreed, so my conditions are met. I wasn't sure whether to read this, or if coming was the right thing to do. Now I'm here, I know it was the *only* thing to do. Anyway, this diary is all I have. What else would I say? Jon agrees, and so I'm going ahead."

He looked around at the viewers.

"I'm glad you're happy to be here, and so am I. But if we're going to do this, then remember it's not a celebration and kindly be respectful. Certainly, it's not about belittling my sister, Devora!"

He glowered at the onlookers, and Anees and I clutched at each other.

"I love him so much," she whispered.

With a thunderous expression, my brother continued. "The Craw war was the worst of times for all factions. Shameful and greedy. No creed acted with more honour or compassion than any other, though many individuals did so. Thousands of people died. *Died*. It's years after, and the word has become letters in a history book. Boasting in a bar. Rubbish that politicians spout."

He glanced towards the facilitator. "Why are we here? Forgiveness by the privileged few who hold the power? We shall see."

I let free some of the tightness gripping my body and heard my brother speak the contents of my heart. I didn't know how he'd come to the same conclusions, but I was proud to be with him and of the same name.

"A death by creed war forms a rip in the universe. Every dolphin and crab feels the loss and what the person might have achieved. We all lose. We bear the shame and betrayal of the *waste*."

Anees sobbed into my hair.

"I love him too," I whispered.

My brother continued without faltering. "People are still suffering from decisions made then. They always will. Nobody thought about the children. About us. I came here for Jon and my family, but I stand for every child who wasn't heard or listened to. For the ones who didn't come through. I can't speak in their place, but I tell you I think about them every day, and I always will. They're not forgotten, and they're watching you today—with your *generosity and kindness*. For them, it's far too late. Where were you thirteen years ago? Where were your grace and long gowns?" My brother spat rather than spoke.

"How much money did you spend on this ceremony today? Pity you never thought of sending money to Exer, where people daily go without. Not once—not once—have you tried to contact us in thirteen years. We wouldn't be here if it weren't for my cousin. Any thanks are down to him, not you. Yes?"

He turned his hands palm up, waiting for questions or comments. When there were none, he began.

"I wrote diaries of my time as a shield boy. When we got to Exer, I hid them under the floor and for many years, pretended to forget. Jon dug those diaries out and made me see. I almost burned them! But I couldn't."

My brother bowed and swayed, and almost, I thought he'd cry. I was wrong. With years of practised skill, he gathered himself up and continued with ever more conviction.

"A few weeks ago, I read them. It ripped me up! There are many things I'd forgotten. It's been so long, and only now I can fully understand the impact of what that time did to us. To me, my cousin, and my sister. To Exers and the other children of the wars. The ripples of hate will never stop until we speak and until we listen."

He stopped for a minute and fought to suppress strong emotion. Anees climbed onto the bench and stood in solidarity with him with both hands held over her chest. My brother glanced across and smiled before continuing.

"I rewrote those diaries for the speak-and-listen. It

wasn't easy. It won't be easy! Don't think you're going to be able to walk away afterwards. Be clear. If you listen to this, you'll be changed."

He rubbed his face with a hand before going on.

"I've altered the names of everyone except my own family. I don't know how best to do this—if I should stop for a break or keep going?"

He looked to the facilitator, but she would give no answers.

"It's your story to tell however you wish," she said.

In the middle of the packed hall, with the world waiting, my brother stood tall as the sea god of waves, Tsunami himself.

"The first time I saw my baby sister, she was a wrinkled up little thing in a blanket. She gurgled, and that was it. I was hers. I loved her with all my heart. I would have done *anything* for her."

He paused to look over at me. "My sister, Devora. I hope this gives you the answers you need."

When he opened the first page, the hall was so quiet you could have heard a grain of sand hit the floor. "The shield diaries."

CHAPTER TWENTY-TWO

AS ONE BEING and one purpose, the people and beasts in the hall listened. Even the bees and birds became still as my brother's words spun a world of darkness and pain. Like rhythmic tides, our hearts beat because it was so. We stopped thinking of ourselves as beings from opposing creeds. We stopped thinking at all.

We remembered the laws created when the city was formed.

The way of Craw is the way of the sea.

Sea Mother protects her children.

Storms kill.

The immense weight of the diaries hit like lead. The truth of involving children in wars was revealed. Many onlookers sat with heads bowed. Some led their children away, and others let them stay. At times a low noise like distant waves would ripple through the rows of seats. The tears flowed freely, and often.

At times, Korl's account was too much for me to bear. I, who had yearned to know all, wished he would stop.

Anees returned to her seat and held my hands throughout. I sensed she'd heard the diaries before and perhaps even helped Korl to rewrite them. She checked on me often with smiles and kisses, and her thumb linked through mine. I took comfort from her closeness and knew I wouldn't have been able to sit alone.

I couldn't remember the Gatehouse or the days of our confinement, yet I knew the account Korl told was true. I couldn't picture us back then, and still, I experienced physical pain. It was as if the ripples and echoes of that time had finally reached me, pummelling with their truths.

Korl's determination didn't waver, sometimes sounding like the man he'd become and at others like a young boy. I smiled at the childish cheek, and Anees did the same.

"He sounds very like you," she whispered.

My brother wasn't alone for long. Jon listened to the first extract and then made his way to the dais, climbed in with Korl, and began to translate my brother's words using the merfolk book they'd made together so long ago.

They looked again like two young boys. Seeing them together; thinking for each other with hands clasped, made me happier than since the day my cousin had left.

When Jon held up the pages to the illuminator belt, I knew he guessed I'd struggled to feel connected to my brother's account. Like so many of his actions, it was for me.

The illustrations brought the diaries to life in a way the

words had not. I wondered if any of the other shield children from the Gatehouse were in the audience with us, and if they benefitted, too, from my brother's painstaking artwork.

I allowed myself to be drawn back to the Gatehouse, visualising the beds we slept on and smelling the damp walls. I remembered how the cold stone of the mermaid statue had felt against my child's fingers.

I remembered the last time I saw my ma and cried bitterly for the years wasted and lives lost. Sobbed like never before. From their rapt faces, it was apparent every person was similarly lost to their own awakenings and regrets. As insignificant pebbles on the beach, we experienced the water of truth when it trickled out and swept us away.

My brother stopped at the end of diary eight and asked for a short respite.

"I—I feel the need to sit with my family before going on," he said. "Just that."

Chapter Twenty-Three

ADU LED ME to a small, secluded garden, exploding with pink and blue flowers. A table lay ready, covered with fruit, drinks, and treats of every kind. When I saw my brother sitting close to Jon, a shattering series of sobs burst forth.

I reached him before he got to me and wrapped myself around him. It was but seconds before the awkwardness vanished, and I truly knew it was my Jon and not a stranger.

Away to the left, my brother and Anees kissed and cuddled and didn't seem to notice us at all.

"My Devi Bee! I'm sorry I didn't say goodbye. If I had, I wouldn't have been able to leave you behind. You looked so old in there, but here—I can see it's you."

My cousin looked healthy and was more rounded than he used to be. His curly hair blew in the breeze, and he talked without using the book. I'd forgotten how twinkly his eyes were and how his cheeks dimpled when he smiled.

"It was the blood, wasn't it? I asked. "The last straw?"

"Not only that. I knew we had to break the cycle, otherwise it would all have been for nothing. I couldn't let us go so easily. I tried to talk with Korl, but he couldn't hear and didn't have hope. Years ago, I started sending adverts out all over the world for people like us. I heard from Adu and Luce. I couldn't forget the shield children and wanted to know if they were all right. The speak-and-listen became a possibility. Not courts as such, but discussion and a new start, where everything is spoken. And—here we are. I hoped you'd come! But I didn't know for sure. When Adu told me she'd received your form, I wept and wept and then made you a cake in the shape of a mermaid."

I cried for a while and counted all the birthday cakes he'd made throughout the years. "Do you remember the whale birthday cake?"

He laughed and nodded. "You could never forget the sea, Devi. More than anyone, you kept it alive. Even when you were young, you were forever talking about fish and seals."

"Not only me. Korl, too, with the mermaids."

"Your ma used to say you had sea for blood. Her name was Shell. Your da was Jula. They loved you. Not all you need to know, but it's the first thing. The most important thing," Jon said.

It was the first time we'd talked about my parents. It was a great relief, and I kissed my cousin heartily. "Is it over now? I'm not sure I can take much more."

He stroked my hair and cried too. "Not yet. There's a lot

to say. I suppose I always knew one day we'd come back to Craw. I feared it would be without Korl and the gangs."

"I'm sorry I couldn't speak in there," I said, then noticed his shirt bore the pattern of koala bears and pineapples. I twisted a button. "This is an improvement."

My cousin stroked my fingers gently. "Thank you. How did you get him to come? I know he wouldn't be here if it weren't for you. He was on a road to destruction, and nothing could get him to see sense. He wanted to protect all the Exers by fighting! Standing up for them in ways we couldn't when we were kids. Honestly, it broke my heart to leave you both."

"It wasn't only me who convinced him. He was thinking about it all along. Making mermaids for the kids and trying to keep things together for the gangs. Also—" I nodded towards the couple engrossed in each other.

"I noticed." Jon grinned. "I'm so pleased they're together. They look so happy."

"I have a girlfriend. Sort of. So much has happened!" I wished the day were over, and we could catch up and have fun. I blew a dandelion at my cousin and told him about Ren, school, Eileen, and Will.

"I see how it is now, Devora," Jon said. "You've outgrown me. Where's my cheeky Devi?"

"You can call me Devi. I'm not even sure I like Devora. I only asked Korl to use it because he refused."

"Not in there he didn't. I heard him say Devora!" Jon said.

"Wasn't he magnificent?"

"Magnificent." Jon laughed. "I can't even say it right never mind spell it. Well, it seems like forever since I left. I want to know everything that's happened."

But it was my cousin who stole the limelight with his own revelation. "I've found someone too. A *special* someone."

"Who?"

He laughed at my astonished face and tweaked my nose. "A Skarle man. You'll see. He's coming to meet you later. Good times are coming, Devi Bee. I know it."

We joined Korl and Anees and ate, and too soon, it was time to go back into the hall. A headache started, and I noticed the gardens had become filled with tiny beach flies.

"A storm is coming," I said. "Can you smell it?"

"A storm, yeah. You could call it so." Korl's eyes locked with Jon's. "Let's get it over, and then we can go back to the cottage and rest. Or run—whichever."

"Korl? Are you ready?" Jon caught my brother and brought him to a stop.

"I hope so." My brother glanced towards me.

"Ready for what? The worst is past." I didn't understand the strain on my brother and Jon's faces. "It'll be fine. It's almost over! I've got your room ready. There's a nice blanket with pufferfish patterns."

"Perfect," Jon said.

We returned to the circle. I believed it was almost done, and the day would come to a ceremonial end quickly.

When my brother started reading anew, the chatter died away. Korl took a deep breath and began his ninth diary entry. When he reached the part where my uncle appeared, something happened to my vision. The hall faded, and all I could see was the shield children waiting for the door to open.

"The door opens.
Uncle staggers in.
Drunk."
I fired his own gun at Uncle. He died," my brother said carefully and with deliberation. "I killed him. *I did it*. My uncle was the Fern leader. After his death, Craw fell and the international armies took control."

My brother gulped. "Many people supported Uncle and his actions, including the formation of shield clubs. Using children in the war effort to confuse the enemy? Maybe some of you? Failing to think about the impact hatred would have on kids— Did *you* do that?"

A muttering went through the audience. My heart rate increased, and I expected to hear horrific details. I wondered why Korl hadn't skimmed Uncle's death as I guessed it was the event he and Jon had so dreaded.

My brother breathed deeply before going on. "His wasn't the only death. Of course not. I've excluded the others. When I read the diaries, I used the word shield. I want you to understand— Sometimes, the item we held was not a shield but *a gun*. I've kept the most horrific details private because of the children listening, and because I don't need to say more. You know what guns do. I'm sharing my uncle's death because—he was *our* family. I don't have the right to share more."

Tears dripped from my brother's face. "His death led to what came next. I *know* the Mainland penalty for killing a leader, even by accident. I know! I won't be allowed back to Exer or Craw. By coming here, I have exiled myself. I realise the consequences of what I'm saying, but still I say it— *I killed my uncle, the leader of Craw.*"

Muttering from the watchers became louder and intrusive, and the officials exchanged rapid discussions. My brother covered his face with his hands. Anees sobbed and wailed. I wished with all my heart we hadn't come to that dreaded place.

The facilitator held up a hand high for silence, and the noise died down.

"No judgement from us, Korl," she said severely. "We listen without casting sentence, or this ends now. Speak, and listen. Our mantra and promise. I knew we would hear of this event—in one way or another. The time for recrimination is gone. For you, but not for us. It is *we* who carry the consequences and responsibility. We were adults. We had all the choices. You did not."

At her words, my brother swooned and collapsed. Anees rushed across, and Jon bent to help him.

"Do you want to stop?" the facilitator asked. "It's too much for one day. Perhaps you need not say anymore?"

"No," Korl said. "I need to finish it, and that's how we'll start to live! For me, for my family, the other shield children, and Exers. If we're starting Craw with a fresh canvas, everything needs to be admitted. It's down to me to do it right."

He pulled himself up. Jon stopped him from speaking and flicked through the mermaid book frantically. Eventually, he put away the book, looked up, and spoke into the voice tunnel.

"Korl's account is not fully true. I shot my father. Major Kraken, the Fern leader of Craw. It was me, not Korl. I killed him. It was an accident, but I accept all blame. His death gave us the chance to live. He would never have allowed us to surrender."

My cousin collapsed into Korl, and they stood united, ragged and brilliant. I would enthusiastically have fought off every member of the audience to keep them safe.

"It's my fault. We didn't know about the bomb—we wanted to get out," Jon said.

"No. It was me."

"No," Jon insisted.

They turned at the same time and looked at me with terrified faces. I sensed Anees's breath quicken, and then she leapt up onto the bench.

"No! It was me. I killed him. I'm responsible. You can dole out any punishment to me but not to the Kraken family."

The three looked directly at me. Still, I didn't understand. The watchers began talking and muttering again. The storm that had been building broke into glittering drops of rain. Soon we were drenched.

The next person to stand was Shena, Ren's ma. From the far end of the hall, she shouted, "I killed the major. If there's any exiling to do, you can do it to me!"

One by one, the people in the hall claimed responsibility for the death of Jon's father and the destruction of Craw and the ocean.

By the time I spoke, the hall was full of people talking, and nobody heard my voice anyway. "It was me. I fired the gun."

The truth was revealed, and I sat back on the bench drained and exhausted.

The facilitator made an impassioned speech about collective responsibility for the atrocity which forced children into killing and thereby took away their human rights.

"The crime was not the death of Major Kraken but of forcing children into situations of war! Starving and imprisoning them. Denying education and love. Taking away consent, and choices. And then—exiling them to a lonely fate across Mainland. A set of grievous crimes and must be atoned for."

At her words, my brother collapsed onto his knees, sobbing. The facilitator got on her knees too. She held my brother's face in her hands and cried with him.

"We must all accept a part in what happens next. I heard what you said about our flowing gowns and privilege. I want to know more, much more. Don't stop talking! Speak! I want equality and options. Opportunities and a future for us all, including the exiled shield children!"

She took my brother's hands. "Do you accept that? Will you stay and help us to shape the future? This is just the start. Under any circumstances—you get to dictate the terms. You speak, and we listen. Then you speak more, and still we listen. What do you say?"

He nodded immediately. "Yes."

"And you?" the facilitator said to my cousin.

"Yes," Jon said.

My brother read the final diary while I sat immobile and empty.

CHAPTER TWENTY-FOUR

HIGH ON THE dais, Anees stood straight with a knife in her hand. When she held out her other arm, a bird swooped down and landed. She kissed it and then spoke upwards, into the sky.

"My future is bound with the Krakens. My name is Anees Loutre. I'm an Ansar. I'm also a Kraken." She placed the knife on the stand.

With her confession, my heart broke. I loved her as a sister and realised how much more difficult her life must have been because of her secret ancestry.

Her voice shook, but she continued on as brave as ever. "I witnessed the balloon leave, and I found my own way of flying across the mountains. With the birds' help, and because of my ancestry, I lived. I love Korl, Jon, and Devora.

I'm going to have our baby."

The bird flew away. Anees placed a protective hand across her stomach, while tears dripped onto my cheeks. My brother's expression didn't change, but he walked across and embraced Anees passionately. It was clear nothing he'd heard was a surprise.

"Thank you for trusting us with your identity," the facilitator said. "What else would you like to say?"

"I wanted to show you something precious with permission from every Exer," Anees said. "They didn't attend today, but they wanted you to know they're also willing to speak, and they look forward to doing so. When Korl gives the word, they'll come all the way through Mainland via train or car. They'll even walk."

With my brother's help, she placed items into the illuminator. Soon the pictures of the Exer tunnels appeared, some black and white, others vivid and coloured. She'd forgotten no one, for I saw my own childish painting flash upon the walls.

Children from the watchers began pointing and touching the illuminations and exclaiming at the graffiti art shining across that place. For a while, the hall buzzed and hummed with laughter and exclamations.

Next up came the statues of Exer, ending with the Kraken mer. When confronted by her spikes and claws, the onlookers gasped and murmured, but I was happy to see her and held up my hand by way of greeting.

Eventually, images filled every available space on the ancient stone walls. Despite their humble beginnings, Exer art easily matched the splendour and dignity of Craw.

The very last picture depicted my brother's filled box of

mermaid figurines, each one with different features and characteristics.

"It was Devora's idea to collect images and evidence. I wanted to show you what the shield children have become," Anees said. "How we took Craw with us and—even though you denied us culture—we claimed it anyway. We couldn't leave our home. It came with us, as roots do. Who can leave their heart? Exers aren't poor victims, needing your rich help! And neither are you saviours. We demand to come back, now, to Craw. Not as criminals but as citizens and equals."

My brother embraced her again. They stood, together and proud, alongside the pictures of our people.

A lady sitting next to Luce, stood and indicated she wanted to speak. She walked before my brother.

Korl recognised her and lowered his head. "I'm sorry. I copied your art for years without asking."

But it was she who bowed lower and took his hands. "My name is Arker Fi, but you already know so. People have asked me to stand as Craw mayor, but I refuse. I will not stand in authority. You might know me better as the Mermaid Artist of Craw. Your work is astounding. I'm right, aren't I? It's your stonework? The Kraken mer is one of yours? And it's you who has been crafting mer for the children?"

My brother nodded. "I know you very well, though it's been years. I met you when I was a child, and I've never forgotten. Never! I started drawing merfolk in the Gatehouse with Jon. From a prison cell, I watched your mermaid vessel in the sky on the day you escaped. I heard you saying you'd come back for me! I knew a light had departed Craw, and it struck a severe blow. When we got to Exer, I was determined never to forget you and your message of hope. I made the mer from all the things we didn't have, and what I could find. With clay from the riverbanks and stolen materials. With hate and regret, and deep sorrow. Over the years, from wishing the children could have a better life than we did. Your mermaids gave me the strength to be kind and still to find love even after what we went through."

My brother held back emotion. "Your merfolk gave us life and hope. It's all we had. Each Exer child has a mermaid. In case today does not go well. In case war comes. Those children will be looking to the sky and waiting for my sign. I've never forgotten what you did for me. For us all."

Arker Fi bowed her head again and crossed her hands above her chest to indicate the honour she felt. When they hugged, tears poured down my cheeks again.

"I'm glad my work kept home alive for you. But your own art is greater because it kept you alive. I would like you to help me restore the stone merfolk to the city and the schools. There is much work to be done. The children need to come back! They need *you*. Will you help me, my daughters Luce and Adu? Our city cannot be restored without the children."

My brother resolutely shook his head. "I'm not good enough. I've done bad things and given way to despair. I didn't know the right path. I'm unsure and weak." He covered his face with his hands.

"And because of your answer, I know you will be perfect. What use have I for people who claim to be strong and sure?" Arker said. "For people who have never known difficulty? It's easy for them to be good, and righteous, and charitable. I don't want those people. I want you—because you've scraped the darkness, yet still you come here today and bare all. *That*—is what I want. I would accept no less. It's no pretty mermaid the world needs but claws and teeth."

My brother removed his hands and looked up with damp eyes and the eagerness of a child.

"Will you come with me?" she asked. "Who better than you?"

"Yes, a thousand times. Yes!" my brother said.

Arker was joined by Adu and Luce, who hugged my brother warmly and tearfully. Afterwards, the facilitator asked for silence and brought the case of the family Kraken to an end.

"Do you want to speak, Jon Kraken, founder of the speak-and-listen?" she asked my cousin kindly.

Jon shook his head. "I wanted to offer Korl and Devi a chance of a better life, and it has been done. I don't have anything more to ask, except that you *promise* Exers are offered citizenship. Korl will bring them back to Craw. For him, they'll return and help rebuild the city. Not to forget what happened, but to make sure it never happens again. There must be a safe place, always, for children of war."

My cousin looked towards me and smiled. "And for children and young adults to be invited to the courts where important decisions are made. To have the same rights as adults."

The facilitator nodded. "Yes, those terms will dictate the new Craw laws. We look forward to you being part of our courts and government. We want to welcome the children and grandchildren back to Craw, not as forgiven criminals or heroes, but as citizens with rights and opportunities. We have no powers over other lands, but we hope others will hear of the speak-and-listen and will follow our lead. *Your* lead. It's time to flood the streets."

She turned to me. "Devora, would you like to speak?"

"Y-Yes," I said, though still, I didn't know what to say.

I made my way to the dais and stood upon the chair facing the image of the Kraken Mer. My papers dropped to the floor, but I held on to the poem Ren had given me and reached into my pocket for my brother's mermaid figurine.

I looked around the hall for Ren. She caught my eye and held my gaze. When she held up a tissue and blew it into the air, I copied and blew back. A gust of breeze caught the tiny white square and took it far away.

"Listen," I told the watching crowds. "I'm still angry. I'm angry! I want to rip down the pretty curtains and set fire to your gowns. *You* get to go home tonight knowing you have done a kind and lovely thing by bringing us here. Lucky you—to feel satisfied and safe and know you had the power. This wasn't our trial—but yours. All adults! It's you who are on trial. We speak, and *you* get to listen."

The people drew a collective breath and went utterly quiet.

Across the hall, the Kraken Mer stared back at me with vengeful eyes, and it was as if Hell looked into a mirror.

I lost my nerve and closed my eyes. A voice very like the one on the sea path hummed and buzzed in my head, saddened, embittered, and wrought with revenge.

When next I dared to look, Anees's hands were placed protectively across her stomach. My family watched and waited. If I asked, they would leave Craw today and never return.

The years faded. I was a little girl alone, faced with frozen faces and clutching a gun instead of the hand of my ma.

I searched the rows for Ren. She understood and made her way through the benches to the dais.

"Didn't I say I'd be here? Speak, Devora. Speak," she said.

I tried and struggled to find a voice to represent both mermaid and gun, beast and girl.

"I thought coming here would be the end, but it's not. I want the speak-and-listen to go on and on and never stop. In schools and colleges, pubs and homes—everywhere! For words to be used instead of guns and knives. I want somewhere to visit my parents and remember their lives without guilt. That's what I want. Maybe I am a monster. It's how it is."

Ren gripped my hand tightly.

I welcomed the sweet release of tears and laughter both. Hand in hand, we rejoined my brother and cousin, exhausted, drained, and happy.

"Was it right? Did I say the right thing? I want us to stay here."

"Well done, Devora. You did good. Really, really, good." Korl and Jon hugged like they would never let me go.

"My brother. My family." I spoke into his ear and held him just as tightly. "You can call me Devi. I don't mind."

"I'm so proud of you," Jon said. "Of us all. We did the right thing."

A din like faraway trains, loud wooshes, whoops, and howls began. It was the storm I'd smelled earlier. People leapt up in fright, and officials ran to see what was happening.

"It's the water pipes," one shouted. "We can't get out!"

"Is it a volcano?" another screamed.

It started with the empty fountain at the far edge of the hall. It croaked and groaned as if in terrible pain. In the final seconds, the screws securing it against the wall burst free. It was water; gushing arcs drenched the watchers and made the children laugh and run into the circle with outstretched hands.

"It's water! Sea Mother invites us back!"

The hall erupted with applause and clapping until a man forced open the locked doors. "The barrier has come down! Lightning has hit the barriers," he shouted.

"To the beach!" the facilitator called.

We spilled from the hall onto the streets where the metallic barriers lay flat upon the ground to reveal a city once again filled with life.

"It was all for me, wasn't it? Because you wanted me to know?" I asked my cousin.

He tried not to agree, but the light of truth shone from his eyes.

"You had to know the truth, or it would have destroyed you like it almost did Korl. Not only the truth of the deed but of the whole, complicated time. We have nothing to be guilty for. If not for the speak-and-listen, maybe Korl would've fought another war in Breen. More children would be hurt. I couldn't let it happen. Not talking kept us safe when we needed it most, but in the end, it devours you. Let's speak, and talk, and never stop. You don't get to talk without someone going first!"

For a while, we hugged, and it was just us two.

"We have a proper home at last, Devi Bee. With the sea,

and talking, and walks together. All the cake you can eat.”

"You were brilliant," Ren whispered shyly. "I knew you'd get it right. I always knew."

I held on to them both as if wind and ocean might sweep them away. Around our cocoon, people laughed and tried to catch rain falling like golden drops of honey. Even the morose guard was happy, with a laughing child gripped in each hand.

"To the ocean! I'll race you," my brother called.

We wound down the city towards the sea. The storm which started with a pair of scissors and a sea gherkin ended on Craw beach. By the time we joined our people, a school of dolphins waited to greet us.

I didn't see who initiated the chain binding us, hand to hand, or who started the chant which would later reach every corner of Mainland.

"When all-a world goes dark, look up,
To find me in the skies.
Close not thine heart,
Or dim thy voice,
Sea Mother, she shall rise."

CHAPTER TWENTY-FIVE

One year later

Dear Eileen and Will,

From one late mermaid to her favourite sea lion and dolphin, sorry-sorry it's taken me so long to write! After my last letter, so much has been happening, and I know you're busy with contracts and packing and such. Time has flown.

Korl said you both looked well in Breen and thanks you for your help with the mermaid transportation. He's still working with Arker, Adu, and Luce, though now the baby's here, he says he doesn't want to miss out and won't leave Craw again. Which is a pity as he's grumpy, ha ha. (Though not so bad as he used to be. Don't tell him I said so, or he'll get a big head.)

We don't know if they'll decide to transport the Exer tunnels back here, too, or if they'll stay in Breen. Nobody can decide. I don't know what's best either. Some days, I think it would be good to see them here, others, that they should stay in Exer. I don't know. Like so many things, it's up to the shield committee. I'm a member, but I only turn up to meetings when there are biscuits.

The best news ever—yes, I'm an aunty! My little niece, Rendre, came in the middle of the night. I can honestly say she's the most gorgeously cute baby ever, and thank gods, she takes after Anees and not my brother (no hairy toes). I've attached a photo. She loves the beach and the sea already. She's got her own bucket and spade, though, her fingers are far too small to hold it yet. And she already has an entourage of baby birds who visit her on the beach and in the garden. When you get here, you get to be honorary auntie and uncle.

Your house is ready. It's right next to us and near the shops. The school is only a few streets away, so when you start work, you can roll out of bed and get there without even brushing your hair (Will).

Ren, Jon, and I have brought in furniture, and Korl and Anees took care of the walls and paintings. I really hope you like merfolk. If not, well, you're going to hate it. I think you'll be happy. It's very comfy and warm, and your garden overlooks ours. The sea flower we planted a year ago has taken off, and now everywhere is covered. I know you'll enjoy it. The flowers open every morning and snuggle shut again at night. When I lean my head out the window every day, they look like a choir singing. It's so sweet!

Everything is ready. There's even a space out front for the bike. I've left you some books I think you might like and a big map of Skarle Island.

Let me know what time you're setting off, and we'll have a meal ready. Jon's boyfriend, Calmar, knows about Skarle food and says he's going to cook you a proper feast, so no need to worry I might poison you. Hah!

I'm so excited to see you! Is it truly a year since I left? These days, people arrive in Craw all the time. It's been great helping them settle in. Some take longer than others. We've worked hard getting the pipes and generators working to full capacity and doing everything we can to open the city back up.

The merfolk school is set to start classes in two weeks' time, and I can't wait. Ren says she doesn't know how she'll be able to concentrate on lessons, and she's forgotten how to write, but it's not true. She's writing more poetry these days and learning to weave.

We've got your office clean. I've even hung the keys up ready for when you start. This school won't need guns or security, but it does need some friendly, kind receptionists. That's you.

I guess you saw the mermaid balloon fly over Breen and Exer? Korl, Arker, Adu, Bluebell, and Luce took her up one last time and have brought her home safely all the way through Mainland to Craw. My brother wanted the children to see her, like he did when we were locked in the cell. Many Exers returned to Craw, carrying the little mermaids Korl made. They waited for my brother's sign as he'd asked.

Now the city is open, there are hundreds of people our age. The beaches are busy again, and I don't just mean on the shore. The ocean is teeming with life. Sea scientists aren't allowed to do anything but look. I know you're going to love being back. How could you not? We've left you a surfboard in the garden, of course. I haven't forgotten our date, Will.

It's taken ages, but we traced every one of the shield children from the Gatehouse. Luce and Adu helped. Bluebell too! Most have chosen to come back and help with making the decisions and councils. Even the one my brother thought we'd lost. He's home now. My brother was right—in the end, he never betrayed the Krakens. When my brother sent word, he came and brought the rest with him. The sea is a stronger force than hate and anger, exactly as you once told me, Will.

There's so much I can't say on paper about water and beginnings and not being guilty. About guns. I haven't got my head back properly, yet. Maybe I never will? I understand, now, why Korl didn't want me to know what really happened and why he and Jon fell out. All those years Jon, Farlo, and all the loyal Exers lived with the fear I'd find out about Craw, and that the knowledge would kill me.

We waited for the mermaids, as the ballad says. Sea Mother rose again, and we won't ever forget or betray the chance she's given us. Last week was the anniversary of the speak-and-listen. I guess you heard how Crawians went down to the beach and sang? And I've heard Mainlanders did, too, and people from all over the world. The oceans everywhere are recovering.

But guns are part of our history the same way merfolk are. Now I know the truth, and there's no need for Korl to hide anything or to be afraid. It won't be sorted quickly or easily. We won't be the people we would have been if the war had not happened. We never had anything to feel guilty about. I see it now.

It's the same with Craw. We left some of the damage as a reminder. There's a house split right in two by the bomb. Cut as neatly as if by a knife. Now, it's a museum piece, an artefact frozen by time.

And we have a weapon museum. Anees started it with her knife, and now there are many sculptures made of knives, guns, and shields. I think it's right we don't pretend they never existed.

The best news is *we talk*. In fact, we never stop! Sometimes we argue and shout, but it's okay. It all needs to come out, and words can cause storms. That's how it is. We talk, and then we listen. Then we talk some more. If we're lucky and it's a good day, all the talking and listening turns into a great big, lovely wave of hearing. I used to believe everything had a beginning and an end. Now, I see talking and listening can be both.

The monster—the real one—didn't come from the sea. It was born of hatred and ignorance, and maybe it'll always be lurking inside humans.

I don't know how to fit all the news into one letter because there's too much, and my niece needs her tea. I'll stop now and will wait for you to arrive so I can show you everything. I can't wait!

Halt the tide and come back very soon because I'm waiting. I'll never forget what you did for us, and neither will Korl.

Your loving friend,

Devi (Devora Kraken). XX

ACKNOWLEDGEMENTS

Thank you: NineStar Press. Elizabetta McKay, for helping me to keep the star aligned and in sight. All of my heart to Maiya, Fazi, Larn, Andrew, Tina, Czeslawa, Chris, Jen, Al, Erk. Also thanks to Loukie Adlem, Sue, and to the gang at the pineapple tunnel.

About Eule Grey

Eule Grey has settled, for now, in the north UK. She's worked in education, justice, youth work, and even tried her hand at butter-spreading in a sandwich factory. Sadly, she wasn't much good at any of them!

She writes novels, novellas, poetry, and a messy combination of all three. Nothing about Eule is tidy but she rocks a boogie on a Saturday night!

For now, Eule is she/her or they/them. Eule has not yet arrived at a pronoun that feels right.

Email
Eule8grey@gmail.com

Facebook
www.facebook.com/eule.grey

Twitter
@EuleGrey

Instagram
@eulegrey

Websites
www.eule8grey.wixsite.com/my-site

www.eulegrey.carrd.co

Snipper-Snapper:

What with dealing with Kitty's kills, and getting down and dirty with surgical body bags, life has never been busier. Keeping a pet is a responsible job, and Mummy completes her duties with pride. She loves being a parent, she does. It's just that the cat flap swishes every time Kitty drags home a mousey. Snipper-Snapper. All day and night, until Mummy is quite frazzled.

Whatever will she do if Amour keeps bringing home the wrong sort of kills? The shag pile can only take so much, and even mummies get lonesome.

CONNECT WITH NINESTAR PRESS

WWW.NINESTARPRESS.COM

WWW.FACEBOOK.COM/NINESTARPRESS

WWW.FACEBOOK.COM/GROUPS/NINESTARNICHE

WWW.TWITTER.COM/NINESTARPRESS

WWW.INSTAGRAM.COM/NINESTARPRESS